The God Zombie

The God Zombie

Nathan Jay

JNJ Publishing LLC

CONTENTS

1 Come With Me 1

2 Emergency 6

3 Attack at the Enclosure 13

4 Arlo's Return 16

5 The Master's Arrival 23

6 The Perfect Choice 32

7 The Army of Hell 45

8 Arlo's Parents 51

9 It's Worse Than the First Time 58

10 Gathering Storms 64

11 Running Out of Reality 67

12 Bob, The Security Guard Who Got Away 77

13 Bob's Fate 82

14 | The House 85

15 | Fortification 90

16 | Parental Rights 93

17 | Indentured Servitude, Maybe 97

18 | A Son's Reprieve 100

19 | Touching the Storm 106

20 | Winding Down 111

21 | The Real You 114

22 | The Strength of the Huturo 119

23 | Sisterhood 123

24 | Recalibration 130

25 | Trespassers 134

26 | Back to the Afterlife 136

27 | Come the Zombies Pt. 1 141

28 | Come the Zombies Pt. 2 147

29 | The Warrior 152

30 | The Lesson 157

31 The Unknown Anger 165

32 Eyes in the Sky 168

33 The Rush to War 170

34 Twisted Reality 173

35 Attack of the Zombies 176

36 The Getaway 185

First Printing, 2023

1

Come With Me

Olivia opened the front door and looked out into the darkness. Although it was night and the weatherman had said the ice storm wouldn't arrive until morning, she could hear pieces of ice hitting the leaves of the trees like thousands of fingernails.

"Weathermen don't know shit," she mumbled, tightening her robe. Olivia stepped out onto the porch and held open the door.

"Come on, Paulie. Potty time."

The golden retriever appeared at the door and looked outside hesitantly. Olivia tapped the side of her leg and coaxed the dog.

"Come on, boy, I know it's cold, but you have to do your business before the storm gets worse."

The dog stepped out onto the porch and suddenly started growling.

"What is it, Paulie?" asked Olivia, walking to the edge of the porch. She looked out into the trees beyond her yard but couldn't see anything. Still, the dog continued growling.

"Is it an animal, Paulie? Is that what you see?"

Suddenly, the dog jumped down the stairs and sprinted across the yard to the forest's edge.

"Paulie! Stop!"

The dog stood growling at something inside the forest. After a few seconds, Paulie began barking loudly and then shot into the woods.

"Shit! Goddamned dog!"

Olivia went back into the house and grabbed a flashlight before entering the ice storm to rescue her dog.

"Paulie! Here boy!" she yelled.

Although it was dark and seeing was almost impossible, the grass was covered in slush, allowing Olivia to follow Paulie's dog tracks by shining a flashlight on them.

"Paulie! It's too cold for this nonsense. Where are you?"

The dog's tracks led Olivia to the edge of the forest, where she stopped—Paulie's prints suddenly were gone. Olivia spun around in circles, trying to find Paulie's footprints but found nothing.

"Paulie!" she yelled. "Here, boy!"

A tree branch snapped inside the forest, and Olivia turned to shine her light inside.

"Is that you, boy?"

Olivia looked for signs of her dog as the flashlight crawled across the foliage. Suddenly the flashlight shined on a pale-faced girl.

"Holy shit!" Olivia screamed, dropping her flashlight to the ground. She immediately grabbed it and hit the switch again, but the light flickered off and on before turning off completely.

"Come on," pleaded Olivia, banging the flashlight against the palm of her hand. But the light wouldn't turn on. Terrified and shaking uncontrollably, Olivia strained her eyes and looked into the forest.

"I'm just imagining things," she whispered.

"Paulie?" asked Olivia inching closer. "Where are you? Come to Mommy."

Suddenly Olivia's eyes fell on a thin shadow lurking next to a large tree. As if sensing the woman, the shadow jerked forward in a clumsy lurch and extended both arms toward Olivia.

Olivia was terrified. She tried screaming, but nothing came out. As the shadow stumbled closer, it cried out in a tortured moan.

"Uhhhhhh . . ."

Olivia finally snapped out of her fear and called out for her protector.

"Paulie! Here! Now!"

Suddenly the dog burst from a large bush and ran to defend the woman. Paulie stood in front of Olivia, lips curled back over his teeth, barking wildly, forcing the shadow to stop moving forward.

"That's a good boy," said Olivia, grabbing her dog's collar and slowly pulling him away from the trees. When she had enough distance between herself and the forest, she turned and started sprinting to the house.

"Paulie! Follow!" she yelled.

The dog barked several times before turning to follow Olivia to the house. They both shot inside, and Olivia slammed the door shut. She immediately turned off all the lights and peered out from behind the curtains at the dark forest, expecting the shadow to emerge.

But nothing came out.

Olivia continued watching for five minutes, then ten—still nothing. Finally, after watching the forest for almost thirty minutes, she turned the lights back on and ensured she'd locked the doors. After one final look at the forest, she turned to Paulie and rubbed his head.

"Thanks for coming to save me. You deserve a treat."

The dog seemed to smile at the mention of a snack and wagged his tail in anticipation. Olivia walked to the cupboard, grabbed the box of dog cookies, and tossed Paulie a treat. Before putting away the box of dog goodies, she walked to the window again and peered into the snowy night—still, she saw nothing at the edge of the woods.

Olivia never saw the dead girl standing just inside the shadow of the forest, watching the house.

Her name was Isadora.

Isadora stood staring at the house, growling and taking in icy breaths, longing to have a piece of her life back. She hadn't accepted her new life entirely. Isadora was a zombie now—an existence filled with unimaginable pain and confusion. There were so many things she didn't understand—how to deal with her rotting flesh and the continuous echoing voices in her head.

Without realizing it, Isadora released another low-pitched moan into the frosty night air. She could feel the cold wind crawling through the open wound on the side of her body, turning her bodily fluids into a slush filled with tiny knives of ice, causing her body to twitch reflexively. Isadora would give anything to feel the warmth of her old bed back at her family's house. But this was her existence, so she had no choice but to try to accept it.

Suddenly a moan rose from beneath Isadora, and she looked down. A body was at her feet; Isadora's ex-boyfriend, Arlo, stared up through the milky white eyes of the dead, frozen tears stuck to his cheeks. In the usual way of living, he didn't have a pulse, and all his organs stopped working. But Isadora knew Arlo could feel pain and was aware of his surroundings.

With spasming arms, Isadora bent to assess the damage to Arlo's body; an enormous hole in Arlo's torso exposed his organs to the elements and sent pulses of pain to what remained of his brain. Arlo's face twisted, and drool dripped from the corners of his mouth.

With her frozen gray hand, Isadora wiped the saliva from his face. She empathized with what Arlo felt because that same pain ravaged her for days when she was changing; losing everything that made her human was so painful that it made her shake. Isadora knew Arlo was going through the worst part of that now; his mind and body were in shock, trying to pull fresh oxygen from the old stale blood in his veins while painful memories of loved ones gnawed away at his heart.

His moans were tortuous cries, and the frozen tears were evidence of his suffering. But it was all irrelevant because there was an ongoing battle between two factions—life and the afterlife. They hated one another and were fighting over which parts of the boy's body belonged to whom. But Isadora knew the truth—Arlo's body belonged to the cold world of the dead, no matter what his brain thought.

The world of the undead was just as confusing to Isadora. She longed to speak regularly but could only control her tongue for simple-syllabled words. Looking at Arlo's suffering, she said what she could to try to comfort him.

"Soon," she said in a deep, scary voice. Her vocal cords, damaged in the unrelenting process of decomposition, made her speech sound terrifying, like a record playing at the slowest speed.

Isadora grabbed her dead boyfriend's cold ankle, and continued dragging him through the forest. She was taking him to the one more knowledgeable than she. The one who'd found her crying in the forest one night, desperate and lonely. His name was Forneus.

2

Emergency

"Can you hear me?" the paramedic asked over the blaring ambulance sirens. "What's your name?"

The boy didn't respond. Instead, he lay on the stretcher staring at the ceiling with a blank expression.

"How many fingers do you see?" asked the man, flashing three fingers. Still, the boy said nothing and continued staring at the roof of the van. The paramedic shined a light into the child's eyes and yelled to the driver.

"This one's lost a lot of blood. His pulse is normal, and his breathing's okay, but his blood pressure is low. He's not responding to any verbal or visual instructions. We might be dealing with a possible stroke or brain trauma. Radio the hospital and tell them to prepare the Medevac."

The driver grabbed the radio and relayed the information to the hospital. When he finished talking, he looked back at the paramedic. "There're two more ambulances tailing us, right?"

"Yeah. They have a boy back there with third-degree burns and one more that's unconscious. What the hell happened over there?"

The driver shook his head.

"I don't know; 9-1-1 just told me it was a multiple-casualty event in the middle of Black Forest. The cops are still pulling out dozens of bodies, mostly kids. Whatever it is, they're keeping quiet about it. The cops on the scene instructed us not to speak to the media, family, or friends."

"Fuck! We're probably going to be working all night. I was supposed to be home an hour ago."

"Yeah, I know. I called my wife to tell her I wouldn't be home until later."

The group of ambulances pulled up to the front of the emergency room entrance, and the hospital workers unloaded the victims. They immediately wheeled the three victims through the hospital and up to the helicopter pad, where a medical helicopter was waiting. Once the patients were loaded, two nurses climbed in, and the aircraft took off.

As the aircraft rose, the nurses began checking their patients' vitals.

"Can you hear me, buddy?" asked Faith.

The child responded by nodding.

"What's your name?"

"Carter."

"Carter? That's a great name. Pleased to meet you, Carter. I'm Nurse Faith."

The child flashed a weak smile.

"Looks like you took a little fall out there, but don't worry about a thing. We'll get you back to feeling better in no time," said Faith, rubbing her patient's head.

Faith moved to the next bed and shined a flashlight on the machines. After noticing the devices weren't responding, she moved close to the subject.

"This one's gone," she whispered to Allison, the other nurse. She quickly stepped in front of the other child's view before pulling the sheet over the deceased child's body.

Faith moved to the third patient, a teenage boy who had sustained injuries to his chest. After checking the machine to be sure his vitals were okay, she lifted the gauze on his chest to look at his wound.

"Huh?" asked Faith.

"What is it?" asked Allison.

"Come look at this," replied Faith.

Allison moved from her patient to Faith's.

"What is it?"

Faith retrieved the patient's medical records from the bottom of the bed before turning to Allison.

"What is this kid's name? John, right?"

"That's what they told me."

"It says here he has lacerations on his face and thorax."

"Yeah, that's right."

Faith looked closer at the patient's chest. "Well, I could be wrong, but . . . there's a lot of blood but no injuries!"

Allison grabbed the chart from Faith and looked it over before moving close to the boy's chest for an inspection. She gently removed the gauze from the chest and shined the flashlight on his skin.

"This has to be a mistake," Allison yelled over the helicopter noise. She carefully ran her fingers along the boy's skin. "Either this boy was injured long ago, or the wound healed itself since the police called it in. Here, run your hand along his chest."

Faith ran her palm along the boy's chest.

"Feel that?" asked Allison. "Isn't that scar tissue?"

"It sure is, but how? It doesn't make sense. Maybe the paramedics got it wrong."

"What about all this blood? From another injury, maybe?"

"The blood is fresh."

"I'm sure there's been a mix-up. This can't be the right patient. Get on the radio and verify with the hospital."

Allison was about to reach for the radio when suddenly her face grew white, and she started moving to the chopper's rear.

"F-F-Faith?"

Faith turned around and covered her mouth in horror—the dead boy's stomach had swollen to the size of a beach ball and was growing larger before their eyes. Soon the sheet covering the dead boy fell to the floor, and the nurses saw the child's stomach, a gigantic black mass that shook as if something were trying to get out. Realizing the boy's stomach wouldn't stop growing, Allison grabbed a scalpel from the adjoining shelf.

"Quick! We've got to cut it before it explodes!"

Just as Allison reached out to make the incision, the boy's stomach exploded, knocking Allison to the floor and spraying black fluid all over the helicopter. A strong, pungent odor rose inside the aircraft, making Allison gag and immediately start vomiting.

"Faith!" Allison yelled, covering her face. "Cover your nose and mouth!"

But Faith didn't respond. Allison raised her head to search for the nurse and found her on the floor, clutching her throat. The explosion had knocked the scalpel out of Allison's hand and sent it flying into Faith's neck.

"Faith! I'm coming!"

Allison grabbed a handful of gauze and ran to her friend's side. "Don't worry, Faith. Stay calm," said Allison.

She quickly removed the knife from Faith's neck and applied pressure with the gauze. Just as she did, Faith lost consciousness.

"Hey! Stay with me, Faith! Don't you go to sleep!"

Allison spotted the handheld receiver dangling from its holder, and she quickly ran over and radioed the cockpit.

"We have a situation back here. Nurse Jerkins suffered an injury, and I need a hand back here. Hurry!"

Allison dropped the phone and attempted to run back to Faith, but as soon as she did, she saw the corpse's open chest cavity. Something within the mound of gooey flesh was moving. Soon Allison saw a head rise in the middle of the pile of meat.

"Jesus Christ!" screamed Allison.

The head started growing, swelling right before Allison's eyes. Suddenly it collapsed on itself, causing pink brain matter to squirt out between the spaces of the undeveloped skull. After a few seconds, the brain matter shot back into the skull, causing the bone to crack and grow. As the head expanded, Allison noticed numerous black sapphire-like objects attached to the bone. As the head grew, the orbs began glowing, sending a high-pitched metallic sound throughout the aircraft. Finally, the round balls cracked open.

"Dear God!" whispered Allison, staring in disbelief. The black objects were eyes! The seven orbs began blinking, displaying a glowing red iris in the center of each of them.

A spine appeared and attached to the base of the monstrous head, while four arms emerged from the mud and attached themselves to the creature. Soon its body formed a massive carriage of skinless muscle sitting atop four powerful legs. Although there was tissue on its bones, Allison could see its beating heart—a glowing mound of muscle that thumped not once but twice per beat, pushing black liquid through its body. Allison fell to her knees and started praying.

"Dear God, my soul is yours. . . ."

But Allison couldn't concentrate because she felt the Demon dog's eyes watching, growling as she prayed. The creature opened its enormous mouth and snapped its jaws at her, slinging thick saliva into her face. Allison quickly wiped it off before turning to Faith; she'd bled out waiting for Allison to save her, but Allison was so preoccupied with the creature that she didn't remember.

"I'm so sorry, Faith," Allison cried. "God, please forgive me."

Finally, Allison's eyes fell on the other patients; John, Allison's teenage patient, tossed aside the sheet and stood while the other child sat swaying back and forth on his bed in a trance. Calm and unfazed by the Demon dog, John moved close to it. As the Hell dog threw its massive head around, John placed his palm on the creature, and the monster fell silent, closing its many eyes.

"What do you want?" Allison asked, trembling with fear.

She could feel John's hatred for her—a hatred born not of confrontation but of her very existence. She felt like a deer being hunted by a predator, knowing death was near and unable to do anything about it.

John continued smiling as he stroked the head of the hungry beast. He slowly removed his palm from the creature's head, and the dog opened its eyes.

"No," whispered Allison.

The dog turned to the child sitting on the bed in a daze and bit into his body. As the enormous teeth stabbed into the boy's body, the child barely made a sound—his eyes closed, an eerie smile on his blood-splattered face as the creature tossed him around. Finally, the demonic dog threw back its head and swallowed the boy while John stood watching, smiling, pleased at the murder he'd orchestrated. Slowly, John turned away from the bloody bed and stared at Allison.

At that moment, Allison saw the sickness in John, the disgusting pleasure he felt from twisting her emotions into knots of fear. He liked seeing Allison shivering amongst the cold flashing lights of the aircraft; John knew he was going to kill her but enjoyed the helplessness that Allison felt of not knowing when her death would arrive.

Suddenly the door to the cockpit opened, and the copilot appeared. "Nurse!" he yelled over the noise. "What is the emergency?" The man looked at the creature on the bed, and his eyes widened. "What the hell?"

He tried to turn around to go back inside, but it was too late. The beast jumped on his back and slashed it open with its claws. Although the man was injured, he tried to alert the pilot.

"Richard!" he screamed, struggling with the beast. "Lock the door!"

The pilot saw the monster, and his face turned white. After watching his friend struggle with the creature on his back, the pilot finally jumped up to lock the door. But before he could snap the bolt in place, the beast opened its enormous mouth, bit off the copilot's head, and sent his headless corpse crashing through the door into the cockpit. As the body sprayed the cockpit with blood, the pilot grabbed the radio and called for help.

"Mayday! Mayday! We have a situation on board! We're going down!"

Suddenly the helicopter started spinning, and everything was a blur of flashing lights and madness. Allison cowered in the corner, screaming hysterically while the monster continued pushing the copilot's body into the cabin. Allison's eyes fell on the red emergency handle that opened the helicopter doors, and as soon as the monster attacked the pilot in the cockpit, Allison dove for the handle and pulled it. The helicopter's side doors opened, and air rushed into the aircraft, pushing Allison in John's direction. Instinctively, she grabbed a cargo strap and pulled herself back toward the open door.

"You're not going to take me, you son of a bitch!" she yelled.

John smiled and continued staring at Allison, unfazed. Suddenly his eyes widened, and he mouthed something to her.

Do it!

Allison threw herself out of the aircraft, and the wind immediately pulled her up into the rotor blades, chopping up her body and sending her head flying back inside the plane. The helicopter stalled, and the rotors started slowing, causing the vehicle to descend rapidly. The aircraft veered left and right before the blades stopped working, increasing the helicopter's descent. Just as the vehicle was about to crash, it froze in midair, inches from the ground.

John calmly walked to the door and slammed it shut. After walking past Allison's decapitated head on the floor, he turned to face the door and opened his mouth—a stream of dark fluid shot out in an endless stream, covering the floor in filth and sticking to the windows and walls. The fluid continued flowing from John's mouth until the helicopter's interior was packed. After a few moments, the helicopter's blades began spinning, and the aircraft rose into the sky, turned toward the city, and flew away.

3

Attack at the Enclosure

Finally, Isadora arrived at a strange structure in the middle of the forest. Exhausted, she dropped Arlo's leg and walked to the building. Isadora could tell it was ancient but was unsure who had built it; the shape was unlike any structure and made it seem like something from a science fiction movie. Although vines and weeds were growing all over it, there were shiny black stones underneath that glowed when hit with moonlight—something Isadora discovered when she stumbled upon it during her transition into the undead.

Isadora looked up and shielded her eyes. The sun was high in the sky, and she could see rays of sunlight penetrating the leaves overhead. Wildlife began to stir, and a deer emerged from behind the building before looking at Isadora and immediately sprinting away. Soon, hungry buzzards started calling out to the other scavengers from the treetops. Several wild dogs started growling from the bushes behind Isadora; they could smell Isadora's and Arlo's decaying flesh, and would soon be there to take their share of their corpses.

Isadora pulled Arlo onto a concrete slab a few steps away from the building and left him there while she stumbled to the entrance. Although she had limited control of her shaking body, Isadora knew she had to hurry and get inside before the animals started attacking. In front of the doorway was an enormous boulder covered in vines that someone had put there long ago. Isadora placed her hands on the side of the stone and pushed until the stone rolled away.

"Uhhhhhh," moaned Arlo from the ground.

Isadora turned and walked to Arlo—he was a mess; his head was black with bruises from his head bashing against objects as she dragged him across the forest floor. Isadora felt terrible, but Arlo's injuries were unavoidable; she hadn't mastered the movements within her clumsy dead body.

Isadora reached down to grab Arlo's ankle, and he started rolling back and forth, trying to escape her grasp.

"N-n-nooooo," he cried.

Isadora understood his behavior and tried to ignore it; Arlo was becoming more familiar with death and was learning to voice displeasure.

There was a rustle in the bushes on her right, and Isadora became more forceful with Arlo, slapping his leg angrily to let him know they were running out of time. The animals were becoming bolder, and it would only be a matter of time before they attacked them.

Under normal circumstances, Isadora would've abandoned the thought of attempting to gain entry—the rock was massive, almost as large as the stone structure itself. But Isadora discovered one positive aspect of the afterlife—unimaginable strength—and she placed her hands on the side of the stone and pushed until the stone rolled away.

Just as Isadora went to grab Arlo's leg, a snarling wolf emerged from the bushes. As it slowly crept close, another wolf walked out from the shadows. Isadora turned to grab Arlo, but a third wolf appeared and began eyeing her. All three wolves walked in a circle around the couple, stalking, threatening, and preparing to pounce.

The wolf closest to Arlo began sniffing rapidly; he could smell the boy's intestines. Unable to keep its hunger at bay, the wolf jumped to attack Arlo, but Isadora immediately grabbed Arlo's leg and pulled him away, sending him flying through the air into the dark building. Deprived of its meal, the dog turned to attack Isadora. The animal released a terrifying growl and jumped, but she quickly grabbed the wolf's throat and tossed it aside. The other dogs hesitated, but only briefly; they were both overcome with the anticipation of feasting on their victim and couldn't control themselves. Finally, they rushed Isadora simultaneously, one clamping down on her bare ankle and ripping away a mouthful of flesh. At the same time, the other pounced on her from behind, biting into her rib cage.

"Off!" Isadora growled, yanking the wolf from her back and slamming it to the ground. She grabbed the wolf at her feet, lifted it, and bit into its back, causing it to scream. But Isadora didn't stop biting—she was hungry, and the bloody wolf meat was delicious. Isadora threw the animal to the ground and attacked, biting off the creature's belly in chunks. As the animal shrieked in pain, she continued biting into its underbelly and drinking its intestinal juices, devouring its insides until her hunger was gone. Finally, Isadora bit into the animal's skull and pried it open to reveal its brain. As she bit into the brain matter and sucked the pink tissue into her mouth, her body trembled in excitement. When she'd eaten the last mouthful, she hungrily looked around the area in search of the other wolves.

The injured animals had witnessed Isadora's ravenous attack and escaped in the brush. Unsatisfied with just one animal, Isadora's dead eyes combed the trees, daring any creature bold enough to attack to come forward. But the forest was silent; the wolves, the birds, and all life was gone. Still hungry and covered in blood, Isadora entered the dark building and pushed the large bolder back into place.

Although the sun was shining outside, the building was pitch black. But that was okay for Isadora because she didn't need light—she could smell Arlo's putrid stench. Isadora walked over, grabbed Arlo by his ankle again, and dragged him through the building. She arrived at a small crawlspace at the rear of the structure and pulled open the small door. After tossing Arlo inside, Isadora sat on the floor and waited in the dark.

4

Arlo's Return

Arlo's body twitched as his eyes roamed the darkness. Although his vision only worked intermittently, he could hear voices around him. Some were speaking to him directly, while others cried out in pain. Arlo realized he wasn't alone. Someone had thrown him into a room with someone—or something; he could feel another presence in the darkness—watching him, enjoying his suffering.

"Isssaaaa . . ." Arlo moaned, attempting to call for Isadora. But he was only able to speak her name partially. He rolled onto his back and tried once again—but this time, a strange, bitter fluid rushed into his mouth, filling it with a chemical taste. Unable to spit the liquid from his mouth, Arlo rolled back onto his stomach and let the liquid drain onto the floor.

In his incapacitated state, Arlo's mind began to wander. He imagined Isadora sitting silently in the corner of the room, watching him suffer. Why wouldn't she help him? What was she doing? Was his pain a joke to her? He imagined his ex-girlfriend playing tricks on him, whispering in weird voices, and laughing. The visions of her mockery soon transformed into anger. He opened his eyes wide and tried to see her. Arlo wanted Isadora to know that he knew about the silly game she was playing. But still, there was only darkness.

Arlo closed his eyes and concentrated. Soon, images of Isadora appeared in his mind. Arlo tried to remember what she looked like but kept running into the same mental roadblock—his imagination kept feeding him images of Isadora as a corpse. Annoyed, Arlo moved his eyes quickly beneath his eyelids to wipe the disturbing images from his mind. He tried imagining what she looked like when they first met, but he couldn't. Next, Arlo tried changing her appearance to something more acceptable; long blonde hair, a curvy figure, and a dress—something Isadora never wore. But no matter how much he tried to alter his memory, the same images of Isadora appeared—a walking corpse covered in blood with a hole in her chest, devouring the carcass of a wild animal in the forest.

Arlo's body spasmed again, but this time something moved across his stomach and toward his heart, a fluttering sensation that felt like something was alive inside him. He tried to run his hands across his chest but couldn't move his arms. Being unable to explore his body felt alien, like he was standing outside of himself, watching the invasion of another person's body. It was an itch he couldn't scratch, driving him mad. It wasn't long before the sensation transformed into something worse—a burning feeling that felt like a butterfly made of acid laid on his chest.

Suddenly, something inside Arlo's chest exploded, and he felt pain throughout his body so strong that he squeezed his eyes closed and started coughing. The sensation in his chest became worse, pressing against his rib cage. His insides burned so bad that dark soot began pouring from his nose and mouth. Arlo knew he was in trouble. He could feel his body temperature rising, and he began to sweat. When Arlo opened his eyes to look around, he couldn't believe his eyes. The room was on fire! The walls, the floor, and the ceiling, everything looked like molten lava in a volcano.

"H-h-help!" he yelled, both surprised and frightened at hearing himself speak. His voice sounded deep and demonic, like a creature from the depths of Hell. Slowly, Arlo lifted himself off the floor. While holding out his arms to balance himself, he took his first step and crashed to the ground. The flames immediately engulfed him, burning his face so severely that all he could do was scream.

"Someone, please help me!" Arlo screamed.

But as soon as he did, the raging inferno blistered his throat and made his tongue sizzle like bacon in a fire. Thick puss rushed into his throat, and he started gagging. The pain was so excruciating that Arlo began to cry—only the sounds coming from his throat sounded terrifying, like a strange creature from Hell mimicking his cries. Suddenly Arlo's entire body exploded in flames.

"AAAAHHHH!" he screamed in agony.

Determined to escape the room of fire, Arlo placed both his hands on the floor and pushed to lift himself again. This time, through unbearable pain, he took small steps toward the fiery wall preparing to use it to balance himself. He reached out for the wall and crashed, hitting it with his head before falling to the ground.

Suddenly on the other end of the room, a small door opened. Arlo looked up to see something pushed in. He heard squealing and instantly knew what it was—someone had moved a wild boar into the room.

"Hey!" screamed Arlo, trying to get the person's attention. But the door quickly closed, and Arlo hurried to the far corner of the room. Through the haze of blazing heat, Arlo looked at the boar; it didn't have the same orange light as everything in the room; instead, the animal appeared normal—all except the animal's head: a deep turquoise blue globe of light encircled its head like a force field. As the animal looked in Arlo's direction, ice crystals fell onto the floor wherever it turned, sending a blast of cool air across the room to Arlo. The animal didn't seem to be affected by the heat at all. Although the entire room was ablaze, the pig wasn't concerned. It grunted a little and then laid its belly on the floor to rest.

Arlo moved closer to the pig, crouching and creeping. He wanted to run to the animal and wrap himself in whatever was making the animal impervious to the heat. Suddenly Arlo fell to the floor and looked up at the ceiling—there was an intense pressure, like someone was pushing down on the building from above.

"What is that?" asked Arlo, cupping his ears.

Still, the pressure increased, rising along with his hunger until a loud metallic noise finally sounded, and blood poured from his ears. Dizzy and unable to understand what was happening, Arlo felt a hunger rise inside him, unlike anything he'd ever experienced. Saliva ran from his mouth like a faucet, and his hands began trembling while his eyes glowed fiery red.

Soon, another smell got his attention, and he lifted his nose and breathed deeply. The odor of pig intestines was thick in the air.

"That smell," Arlo growled.

The aroma of the pig's intestines made Arlo's tongue shoot from his mouth and thrash around wildly; he started biting at the air and, eventually, his teeth clamped down on his tongue, but Arlo didn't notice. All he could think of was the animal's flesh.

"Please, I want it," Arlo cried. As he started moving toward the animal, the boar became afraid and squealed.

"I want to eat. Please," begged Arlo, his hunger making him crawl faster toward the boar. He could hear the animal's heartbeat, a rapid *thump-thump* that filled Arlo's eyes with tears. He longed to listen to the animal squeal while he tore away its flesh and drank its sweet blood.

As Arlo moved closer, the sight of the animal's brain—a pink tissue mass encased in a halo of blue light—came into view and made the inferno in the room peripheral. Arlo instantly forgot the odor of the animal's intestines and became mesmerized by its brain. The blood inside the boar's brain matter looked like pink ice crystals circulating with each heartbeat, calling out to Arlo in a loud, strange humming sound that only he could hear.

The sound was too much for Arlo, and he couldn't resist his hunger.

"Mmmmmm," he moaned in a demonic voice.

Filled with an uncontrollable hunger, Arlo sprinted across the room, jumped on the pig, and bit off one of its ears. The boar squealed in pain and tried to defend itself by latching onto Arlo's arm, but it was no match for the teenager's hunger-fueled superhuman strength. Arlo snapped the pig's neck with one arm and sank his teeth into the creature's head, sending blood spraying in all directions. He chewed through the skin until he reached the skull's hard bone and, like a can opener, pulled the bone away with his teeth until the brain was accessible. Arlo hungrily ran his tongue along the top of the pig's brains and screamed in delight; the ice crystals in the animal's brains weren't ice but shards of sugar, making the brains taste sweeter.

"P-p-pleeease!" Arlo screamed. "Moooorre!"

Like a wild animal, he began scratching, clawing, and biting to peel off the animal's skull. As soon as he removed the bone and the brain lay exposed, Arlo hungrily thrust his face into the brain matter. Swallowing the bloody mess sent an icy sensation through Arlo's center, and he fell beside the animal's body, unable to move. His eyes roamed the room, and he noticed the fire was gone. There were no burning walls or molten floor—only him and the boar carcass, lying in darkness.

Suddenly, the door on the room's far end opened, and Isadora entered. She walked across the room to Arlo and stood over him. A voice rang out in Arlo's head, startling him and causing him to jump in surprise.

"Can you hear me?"

Arlo looked up at Isadora in shock—her mouth wasn't moving, but he could hear her voice in his head. He tried to respond, but as soon as he started trying to form the words, Isadora slapped her bloody palm over his mouth.

"Speaking with your mouth is too difficult. It's best if you try speaking to me with your mind."

Arlo closed his eyes and concentrated. *"Hey. Isadora, can you hear me?"*

Isadora tried smiling, but her decaying muscles prevented her from making the expression. *"Good. You're a quick study!"*

Arlo appeared disoriented. *"What happened to me? How did I get here?"*

"We're dead, Arlo."

"Dead? What do you mean?"

"I mean, we're both dead. We don't breathe the same air as the living."

Arlo sat up, and his body jerked uncontrollably. *"Dead?! But how are we able to move?"*

"We're not dead in the literal definition of the word. We're only dead according to science. The technical term for what we are is 'undead.'"

"What?! Those things don't exist!"

Isadora attempted to chuckle, but her damaged vocal cords made it sound terrifying.

"Didn't you just eat the brains of a pig? What about the fires? Did you see those? How would you classify those things?"

"But . . . if I'm dead, what about my mom? My dad?"

Isadora fell to her knees beside the dead animal and stuck her fingers into its empty head.

"You did a pretty good job on this boar. Nobody showed me how to do anything when I first turned. The first couple of days, I ate possums and rats. Trust me. Pigs are much tastier."

Arlo sat on the floor, staring at Isadora, unable to respond. He watched as she shoved her fingers into her mouth and licked the brain residue off her fingers. After attempting the act once more, she ripped open the pig's belly, grabbed a handful of intestines, and started eating. As Arlo looked on, ashamed of his weakness, she pitied him and placed a bloody hand on his leg.

"You're going to have to come to terms with this, Arlo. We're dead, and nothing's going to change that. We were both tricked by that son of a bitch."

"Who?"

Isadora held up a long strand of guts and let them fall into her open mouth.

"John."

Hearing Isadora speak the name triggered something in Arlo's head, and suddenly a flood of memories came rushing back.

"John . . . I remember."

Soon the memories were everywhere. Arlo remembered chasing the ghost child to the house and descending into the black cave. He recalled the torture room and the numerous prisoners held in cages. And then Arlo remembered the worst part.

"Mani," he said, tears welling up in his eyes. *"He betrayed me."*

Arlo remembered turning around after the knife stabbed him in his back to see his best friend holding the blade.

Isadora pushed the empty pig carcass aside and stood up.

"Come on. It's time I introduced you to the one that saved me. You're probably boring him with your tears."

Arlo tried wiping the tears from his face, but he still couldn't control his shaking hand. *"Who?"*

"His name is Forneus. Maybe you haven't noticed, but he's been in the room with you all along."

Arlo looked around the room, but the faint light entering through the cracked door wasn't bright enough for him to see anything. *"Where is he?"*

Isadora released an evil chuckle that echoed through the room. *"He's lying on the floor in front of you. Forneus is the pig—you ate his brains."*

5

The Master's Arrival

As the helicopter approached the children's hospital, a team of nurses with medical equipment stood waiting on the edge of the helipad while several security guards surrounded the area with weapons aimed. Bob, one of the security guards, looked back at the nurses in frustration.

"Are these patients from the Black Forest accident?" he asked.

A short, chubby male nurse named Oliver responded. "Yeah. The victims are being filtered to us from Tress Hospital because this hospital specializes in care for kids. But with the number of injured, I'm not sure we'll be able to accommodate so many of them."

"How many are there?"

"This flight only has three, but we're expecting over fifty by noon tomorrow."

Bob looked surprised. "Fifty?! Kids?"

"The investigator on the scene told us they're still pulling the injured out of the forest."

"Jeez. What the hell happened over there?"

"Nobody knows. The hardest thing will be to locate all the parents."

Bob lowered his weapon long enough to grab a stick of gum from inside his jacket and shove it into his mouth before tossing the wrapper onto the ground. "How did so many kids sneak out of their houses?"

Oliver shrugged. "I don't know. Poor parenting, I guess. But kids nowadays are sneaky, and I'm sure none of them told their parents where they were going."

Bob shifted the butt of the weapon back into his shoulder and aimed at the aircraft. "I wish my daughter would try that shit. I'd lock her ass up forever."

Oliver chuckled and shook his head in disagreement. "You'd probably be in the dark, like all the other parents. I mean, that's the definition of sneaking out, isn't it?"

After circling the hospital twice, the aircraft hovered above the landing pad and slowly touched down. Expecting the engine to stop and the doors to open, the nurses pushed their stretchers closer. But after a few moments, the chopper's engines continued running, and no one came out.

Oliver turned and yelled at Bob over the aircraft noise. "Why aren't they opening the doors?"

Bob lowered his weapon and moved closer to look inside the aircraft—a dark black silvery substance was coating the windows, and he couldn't see movement inside. Bob sensed something was wrong and motioned to the other guards standing behind the nurses to move closer. The guards encircled the chopper and motioned for the nurses to move back.

"Hey, Bob!" yelled one of the guards from the far side of the helicopter. "You see that stuff on the windows?"

"That's weird. What do you suppose it is?" replied Bob.

The guard moved closer and hit the helicopter's door with the butt of his rifle, sending tiny ripples across the glass.

Bob backed away. "Nobody move!" he yelled over the noisy rotor blades. "Something's on the windows!"

Oliver moved in closer to get a better look. "Hello!" he yelled. "Can anyone hear me?"

But still, there was no movement.

Suddenly the hospital doors opened, and a tall woman with long gray hair walked out.

Oliver immediately went to her side.

"What the hell's going on?" she asked Oliver.

"Hello, Dr. Hansley. We've been waiting for someone to open the door, but there's been no response. Also, there's a strange substance on the windows," replied Oliver.

Dr. Hansley moved closer and looked at the windows of the aircraft. "Oil, maybe?" she asked.

"Could be," replied Oliver.

Dr. Hansley turned to one of the other nurses. "Go inside and contact the Hazmat unit. We may need their assistance."

The nurse ran into the hospital, and Dr. Hansley turned to Bob. "Did you guys try knocking?"

"Yeah, and there was no response."

"Try again. The pilot's the only one who could've landed this thing."

Bob moved close to the helicopter and hit it twice with the butt of his rifle. "Hey! Can anyone hear me?" he yelled.

Suddenly a loud thump banged against the base of the helicopter, and the guards all took a step back.

"You hear that?" asked Bob.

The helicopter's engine suddenly turned off, and everything was silent.

Bob turned to Dr. Hansley. "What do you want us to do? We can wait until Hazmat arrives, but that'll be a while. I don't know the status of the patients onboard, but waiting won't be good for them."

Dr. Hansley lowered her glasses and rubbed her eyes. After a few seconds, she turned to Oliver. "You guys get those stretchers ready."

Oliver motioned to the two nurses standing at the doors, and they wheeled the stretcher onto the tarmac.

Dr. Hansley turned back to Bob. "We don't have a choice. Those patients could die. Go ahead and break the lock."

Bob knocked on the helicopter once more with his rifle. "Hey! Can anyone hear me?" After hearing no response, Bob jerked on the door handle. "It's not opening."

Bob smashed the butt of his rifle on the lock and yanked again, but the door didn't open. Two other security guards took turns banging on the door with their rifles, but neither could enter the aircraft.

Frustrated, Bob turned to Dr. Hansley. "We'll probably need a blow torch to get inside, and we don't have one handy. We can call out to get one here, or enter another way."

Dr. Hansley looked annoyed. "Another way? What are you trying to say? That's a ten-million-dollar piece of equipment."

"Well, you want to save those kids' lives inside, don't you?"

Dr. Hansley sighed and turned away. "Alright, do what you have to do."

Bob motioned to the guards, and the group moved to the front of the helicopter. "Break the glass," he said to the nearest guard.

As soon as the guard lifted his weapon, an explosion sounded inside the aircraft. The blast's force sent the helicopter door crashing into one of the nurses and sent her sailing over the protective fence surrounding the roof.

Everyone stood frozen in shock staring at one another. Eventually, everyone ran to the edge of the building and looked below.

"Holy shit!" yelled Bob.

"Danica!" cried Oliver.

"Jesus Christ! Is she alive?" asked Dr. Hansley, avoiding looking down.

"I don't see her in the street. Maybe she landed on a balcony," said Bob.

The remaining nurses ran into the building, leaving the security guards and Dr. Hansley alone on the rooftop. Bob turned away from the roof's edge and aimed his weapon at the helicopter. Slowly, he crept to the side of the aircraft and looked inside.

"Doc!" yelled Bob.

Dr. Hansley moved closer and stared at the helicopter in disbelief. "Oh my God! What the Hell is that?" she asked.

Although the door was open, a transparent black jelly-like liquid wall stood as a barrier. Inside the fluid were several bodies—two adult males, a nurse, two children, and five strange doglike creatures.

The doctor continued staring into the thick jelly. Suddenly she doubled over and vomited on the roof. Bob was about to comfort her when he lurched forward and threw up. Soon everyone on the rooftop was vomiting.

"What . . . what's that smell?" asked the doctor, wiping her mouth.

Bob covered his face and backed away. "It's coming from the helicopter. I think you'd better call Hazmat, fast!" he said. Bob raised his hand to wipe his mouth and suddenly dropped his weapon. "Doc?" he asked, staring at his hands. On his skin were thick, black, puss-filled sores. The sight of the spots on the backs of his hands made his whole body start itching, and he began walking toward the hospital door.

Soon, another guard screamed and dropped his weapon. "W-w-what the hell is this?" the guard yelled, looking at his hands.

Dr. Hansley raised her hands and saw the same black sores on her palms. "Officer!" she yelled to Bob. "Stay right where you are! Nobody enters the hospital until we know what's happening."

Bob looked at Dr. Hansley and then at his hands. The sores were moving up and down as though they were breathing. "Fuck this shit!" he yelled, and took off running into the hospital.

Dr. Hansley looked into the aircraft and froze. "Dear God."

Standing in the center of the black glob of jelly was the figure of a boy. His eyes were glowing, and there was a strange smile on his face. Although the boy was stationery within the fluid, the other bodies were floating around him as if he was the eye of a hurricane.

Suddenly the dogs' bodies began thrashing, and Dr. Hansley could no longer contain her terror.

"AAAAAAHHHH!"

The strange creatures tore and struggled within the liquid, their limbs growing larger, their enormous teeth pushing out of their mouths. One of the animals bit into the child, and Dr. Hansley screamed again —finally realizing that the child was a corpse with a massive hole in its torso.

Suddenly the dogs all turned to face Dr. Hansley, biting at her, clawing, and pushing their way through the putrid jelly. The creatures drew close to the edge of the sticky substance, Dr. Hansley finally realized they were going to attack her. She took off running to the door, but it was too late. The first wolflike creature burst from the aircraft and jumped on her back.

"Somebody! Help!" she screamed.

The remaining guards looked at the wild dog and began backing away. As the creature bit into Dr. Hansley's neck, the other officers ran inside the building, leaving the woman to fend for herself. Unable to withstand the attack, Dr. Hansley collapsed on the ground, unconscious. With one motion, the creature lifted its enormous paw, decapitated the doctor, and began sucking blood from her neck.

Suddenly all the black jelly melted and poured out of the aircraft onto the hospital's roof. The creatures bolted out of the helicopter and sprinted toward the hospital door. Unable to run inside, they banged against the door until they tore it from its hinges. As soon as the door opened, the creatures backed away, turned to face the helicopter, and lowered themselves to the ground. After a few moments, one last figure walked out of the aircraft onto the hospital roof—it was John.

Covered in black ooze and reeking of human waste, John ambled toward the hospital door. He could feel the evil in the air all around. His naked body, muscular and glistening in the flashing lights of the launchpad, trembled in anticipation. He paused to look up into the sky and smiled—an enormous thunderhead rumbled from above, signaling the next phase of his plan. He could feel the evil bubbling inside him, pushing to cover the world in Hell's filth.

John walked to the entrance, and all the wolflike beasts began trembling and crying as if he'd disciplined them. Enjoying his display of power, John moved through the door and into the building. He walked down a short staircase and entered an elevator. Without pressing any buttons, the elevator doors closed and descended.

When the doors opened, John walked out and stopped; in a large dark room were dozens of children. Some kids wore plastic bands on their arms, indicating that they were hospital patients. Other children wore the sweat of travel on their brows, having walked to the hospital on foot. But they were all there with the same trance painted on their faces and evil glowing in their eyes.

Scattered on the floor beneath them were the bodies of the hospital staff. Their faces told the story of the horrors they faced when the children had accosted them. Some of them had grotesque expressions of pain frozen on their faces. Others closed their eyes in an attempt to pray away their fates. But death inevitably came to all victims through an abundance of suffering—some had their arms ripped from their bodies while others had to endure the tiny hands of their murderers ripping holes in their torsos to pull their intestines out. All were alive when evil disemboweled them, just as John instructed. But none could withstand the damage. In the end, only one escaped their wrath—a security guard who shot his way out of the hospital. But it was of no consequence. Death would eventually come to them all.

The children flocked to John as he stepped over the corpses and moved through the room. They all wanted to touch him, to be a part of him. None of them made a sound, but they all longed to do his bidding, eager to sacrifice their bodies to construct his new world.

John reached out and touched the head of several children as he passed them, sending the lucky few into uncontrollable spasms of delight. As pure evil coursed through their tiny bodies, the children collapsed, shaking uncontrollably atop the dead bodies. Soon each child John touched began transforming. A strange, disgusting disfigurement appeared—the kids' faces grew puffy, like sponges, and enormous teeth pushed through the skin of their chins, turning each of them into strange, hellish creatures. Proud of their transformations, John left the room with an eerie smile.

John walked down a long hallway with flickering lights and paused in front of a set of doors. After reading the words *Operating Room*, he pushed open the doors and entered. Hanging from the ceilings and stuck to the walls were the intestines of the hospital workers. The rank odor of human waste and the metallic aroma of blood made John's heart pound in excitement. A naked, obese, middle-aged man lay on the table with various instruments attached to his face. John smiled as he stood over the body, admiring his children's work. There was a spark of red light in his eyes, and he saw the events replay in his mind:

The patient had been in the middle of a heart operation when the room filled with John's children. The doctor yelled at the kids to leave the room, but they didn't listen. They quickly overcame the doctor, grabbed a scalpel from the tray, and plunged it into his eyeball. The nurses tried running out of the other set of doors, but John's children stood waiting as soon as they opened them. They fell upon the nurses, and while several kids held the nurses down, the others pushed their hands into the nurses' bellies and pulled their guts out. With the doctor and nurses dead, several children walked to the fat man lying on the table. They were confused by his drugged state of sleeping. They could see his heart beating, but he wasn't moving. Finally, one of the children pushed his hands into the man's stomach and grabbed his intestines. But still, the only thing that moved on the man was his beating heart in his open chest. One of the children became frustrated and ripped the man's heart out of his chest. The child held the muscle in his hand, watching it, waiting for it to stop beating. The heart moved in the child's palm a few more times and eventually stopped beating. Satisfied that he'd done his master's bidding, the boy threw the heart across the room. It landed on the floor and slid into a corner.

Suddenly the lights in John's eyes returned to normal. He waved his hand in front of the corpse, sliding it off the table onto the floor. John's body floated, moved over the operating bed, and lowered on the blood-stained sheets. After a few moments, John closed his eyes.

"Oh, Dark One, I call out to your spirit in Hell. Come to me."

6

The Perfect Choice

Arlo sat on the floor, looking at the pig's corpse, expecting it to move, but it didn't. He shot a look of disbelief at Isadora and spoke to her in his mind.

"You're kidding. Are you trying to tell me this boar was a person?"

Isadora looked at Arlo and tried smiling, but her rotting, disfigured face made the expression seem terrifying, and he looked away.

"I didn't get it at first, either, but you'll catch on. Forneus is here," Isadora whispered inside Arlo's head.

Something stirred on the other side of the room that got Arlo's attention, and he jumped.

"W-w-w-ggggrrr," he said, attempting to ask what was there. But he had little control over his dead tongue—it felt heavy, like trying to speak through a mouth filled with clay. Frustrated, Arlo repeated his question in his mind.

"What's that?"

Suddenly the voice of an old man spoke inside his head.

"You can accept your new reality or try fighting against it. But no matter what you do, your life is gone. Your new existence is in the world of the dead, and there is no escape."

Arlo tried searching the room, but his eyes wouldn't focus. His head disobeyed his mental commands—when he turned to look in one direction, an uncontrolled spasm jerked his head in a different direction. Still, Arlo tried his best to search for the owner of the voice in his head.

"Who said that? Who's there?"

"I am Forneus."

Arlo saw a small glowing circle in the center of the wall on the other side of the room. The fire ring grew brighter until the wall burst into flame. Terrified, Arlo slid along the floor until he was against the wall on the opposite side of the room. He watched the fire climb the wall, and a terrifying feeling shot through him. Arlo remembered feeling trapped in the heat of the first fire. The memories of his burning flesh were still bright in his mind—he could still smell the stench of his charred skin and singed hair in the air. He remembered the helplessness and inability to distinguish between hot and cold, that unrelenting pain coursing through his body, making every nerve scream.

"Please, no. Not again," Arlo cried inside.

Arlo lifted himself from the floor with weak arms, stood up, and started swaying uncontrollably before crashing back to the ground. The open wound on his chest that exposed his ribcage slammed against the floor, sending a loud cracking sound echoing throughout the room.

"AAAHHHH!" Arlo screamed in a gravelly, tremoring voice. The injury to his ribs was so bad that he rolled over onto his back and grabbed his chest, an action he immediately regretted after he felt the slimy insides of his chest cavity. Arlo looked up and saw flames covering the ceiling above him. Feeling the heat rising, he closed his eyes and prepared for the fire to overtake him while Forneus continued speaking.

"Yes, yes. For the dead, the degradation of the body torments. Until decomposition has taken your flesh, you will continue to experience the pain of this deteriorating physical existence."

Overwhelmed with fear, Arlo looked around the room for Isadora, but she was gone.

"Isaaaa," moaned Arlo, his echoing voice unrecognizable and terrifying. But he was still unable to form words with his mouth. Arlo closed his eyes and yelled inside himself.

"Where are you, Isadora? I need your help!"

The old man laughed, sending a horrible echo throughout Arlo's mind.

"There is no need to be afraid. I'm not here to hurt you. Isadora is out in the forest, searching for sustenance. In addition to the regular feasting that must occur to replenish energy, there is another food the dead must consume—the soft tissue inside the skulls of the living."

"What? You mean . . ."

"That's right. Eating the brains of the living is the only way to suppress the burning from the Sun Oil. No one knows why but a brain not more than four hours dead has special properties that extinguish the flames. Consuming brain matter once a day allows you to exist, but failing to take your fill will result in the fires returning."

The bright flames crawled across the ceiling and down the wall in front of Arlo. Feeling the heat on his face made Arlo furious, and he tried to yell.

"W-w-w . . . gggggghhhhh . . ."

The old man laughed at Arlo's attempt at verbal confrontation.

"We all hate the burn of the Sun Oil—that is what they call it. But all the undead must suffer within its flames because Heaven and Hell are angry at your existence. Good and bad is an eternal equation of judgment that you've disrupted. You've deprived them of a soul. I know what the churches teach; Heaven is the opposite of Hell, and vice versa. It's mostly true, except for this one thing—Heaven and Hell hate the living dead equally. It is the only thing in the history of their war against one another in which a documented collaboration exists. Together they created a fire that both burns and freezes, casting unrelenting suffering onto zombies' souls until they submit. Either you delay it by eating the brains of the living, or the fire burns you until you are truly dead and presented for judgment.

"The ability to speak through the breath of life is fading. Soon your body will be one with death, and you will lose your ability to communicate with the living—their language will move beyond your comprehension.

If you try hard, you can say a few words, but eventually, the blood in your veins will transform into the sludge of the dead. The poison wipes your memory clean of all you remember from your life, reducing the only remnants of your vocabulary into the sounds of hunger and pain."

"You're a piece of shit and a coward!" Arlo yelled inside. *"Why won't you show yourself?"*

Suddenly an enormous breeze tore through the room, knocking Arlo onto his back and extinguishing the flames on the walls.

"Perhaps I was wrong to bring you back. Maybe it would be better to let your corpse rot in the dark caverns of Black Hills."

"Isadora brought me back, not you!"

Forneus's voice boomed inside Arlo's head: *"Isadora is but a child caught in the winds of confusion. Neither of you could navigate the valley of death without an experienced hand illuminating your path."*

Arlo snickered at the comment. *"And you still haven't revealed yourself. So much for the illuminating path stuff. From what I can see, you're nothing but a voice, too chickenshit to leave your hiding place."*

Suddenly all the walls in the room burst into flame, and the ground started trembling. Arlo tried moving away from the fires by pushing himself along the floor to the center of the room.

"I'm sorry. I didn't mean to . . ." said Arlo, realizing he shouldn't have antagonized Forneus.

Suddenly the wall exploded, sending chunks of concrete and debris through the room. Arlo tried throwing up his arms to protect himself, but he was too slow, and the rocks crashed into his face. After the stones stopped falling and the smoke cleared, Arlo turned to face what was left of the destroyed wall and started trembling at what he saw.

The destruction of the wall revealed a hidden room filled with human bones. Most of the skeletons were still inside their clothing when they met their demise, while others were only bare bones, armless and headless, torn apart by decomposition. An enormous skeleton sat propped up against the wall with the bones of small animals scattered on its lap. It looked massive compared to the other human bones, like it was the remains of a giant.

But what scared Arlo most about the enormous bones was that they were much different than anything he'd ever seen. The skull was a translucent material that allowed Arlo to see what was inside—thousands of tiny glowing worms splashing around in what resembled lava. Seeing the creatures made Arlo's skin itch; he could hear the worms shrieking as they splashed inside, burning in the molten liquid. Arlo put his hands over his ears, but he could still hear their screams.

"Uhhhhh," Arlo moaned in his physical voice.

Arlo looked closer at the colossal skeleton. Tucked inside the skull's eye sockets were two gold coins with holes drilled in the center that looked like eyes. All the teeth were black as onyx except its front teeth—two long golden incisors extending out of its mouth like two spikes.

"Are you a vampire?"

"I am not a parasite!"

"What are all those animal bones surrounding you? Didn't you eat them?"

Suddenly the skeleton brushed aside the bones on its lap and stood, banging its head into the ceiling. It made a fist and punched angrily at the roof, shaking the whole building before lowering itself to walk into the room. Arlo gasped when he saw the rest of the creature; thick glass encased the skeleton's chest, and inside were dozens of white snakes, slithering and biting at one another, trying to escape.

The skeleton's laughter echoed in Arlo's head. *"Does my appearance frighten you?"* he asked.

"No," lied Arlo, dropping his eyes to the floor. *"Are you Forneus?"*

"I am he. Do you continue to deny my existence?"

Arlo raised his eyes to look at the skeleton hovering over him. *"No,"* he answered flatly.

Forneus moved his face close to Arlo's before grabbing him by the throat and lifting him off the ground. As Arlo struggled to free himself, the gold coins in Forneus's head started glowing, and he moved closer, pushing the scent of old death into the boy's face.

"Doubt my power at your peril, foolish idiot," he said, releasing his grip on the boy and dropping him to the floor. Arlo lay on the floor, gasping for air as he watched Forneus walk to the other side of the room, grinding his skull on the ceiling. When Forneus reached the other side, he sat down on the floor.

"What are you?" asked Arlo, grabbing his neck.

With his enormous hand, Forneus scooped up the remains of the dead boar and threw it against the wall, splattering blood on Arlo's face.

"I am the one who will not suffer the questions of fools."

Arlo was silent for a moment before speaking again. *"I didn't mean to make you angry. I only want to understand you."*

Forneus grabbed the head of the pig from the floor, jabbed one of his boney fingers into the creature's eyeball, and popped it out. While looking at the eyeball stuck on his fingertip, the coins in his skull grew brighter, illuminating the room. Forneus flicked the eyeball in Arlo's direction, and it rolled to a stop in front of the boy.

"I am all that remains of an empty man."

Arlo waited in silence. He wanted to ask Forneus many questions but was afraid to do so.

"I can smell the fear inside you, and it stinks," said Forneus, grinding his teeth.

"I'm just nervous," explained Arlo. *"I don't want to make you angry."*

Forneus chuckled. *"You are not as stupid as you appear to be."*

"How did you become what you are?"

"I became what I am through pain."

Feeling more brave and calm, Arlo tried to find out more. *"Will you tell me your story? How did you come to be?"*

Forneus let his enormous head fall back against the wall, sending a loud thud echoing through the room. The impact of his skull hitting the concrete sounded like a bowling ball bouncing on the floor.

"When death comes, and the final breath of life leaves, all souls fall into a deep sleep, waiting for the trumpets of Heaven to awaken the dead for judgment."

"Judgment Day. Yes, that's what they taught us in church."

"Death was different for me. Hell destroyed my mortal life and turned Heaven against me."

Arlo was curious. Although Forneus terrified him, he could sense the sadness in his old voice. *"Were you betrayed like me?" Arlo asked.*

"When a ship traveling on life's ocean crashes and sinks, it's always on the rocks of betrayal. And so it was with me."

"How were you betrayed?"

Suddenly there was a flash of light, and the snakes inside Forneus's chest turned black and stopped moving. Forneus opened his gigantic mouth, and a big sigh escaped him.

"There is not a day that passes in which I don't think of Thema; her smile haunts me."

"Thema? Who was she?"

"She was my wife, partner, and my friend."

The red liquid inside Forneus's glass skull started bubbling, and the worms inside his head started screaming again, making Arlo cover his ears. Forneus lifted his skeletal hand, rubbed it across his glass skull, and groaned. He inhaled again and, gradually, the worms stopped screaming.

"One day, my pregnant wife, Thema, and I went to the Maletsunyane Falls to watch the sunset. We knew the baby would be arriving soon, and Thema begged me to take her there one last time to pray for a healthy boy. We sat on the falls, watching the sky explode in colors. We talked about our future together. We both wanted many children and were happy to receive God's permission to start our family. As I lay on the warm grass, staring into Thema's eyes, I felt a deep peace that I'd never known. It was the most beautiful sunset I'd ever seen. Seeing the sun dancing in Thema's eyes, feeling the rays of the evening sun warm her dark brown skin warmed my heart. I just knew we would be together forever."

Suddenly Forneus grabbed his right hand with his left, twisted it, and jerked it off his arm. He moaned in agony after removing the appendage and angrily slammed the bone to the ground, shattering it. Forneus held his empty wrist up and watched as a tiny thread of nerves appeared, stretching upward out of the bones of his wrist like the roots of a tree. Arlo watched in surprise as the small group of veins expanded, growing larger until he could see five *human* fingers on the wrist of bones. Soon, an adult human's hand, complete with skin and bones, appeared on Forneus's wrist. As Forneus opened and closed his new human hand, it suddenly turned back, and all the flesh fell onto the floor in front of him, leaving only a skeletal hand. Forneus continued telling his story.

"Just before the sun disappeared, one of Hell's Demons found us. I tried to kill that bastard, but the powers of Hell were with him. He tortured me for hours. He used a knife glowing with the fires of Hell to cut the skin from my skull. By the time he finished, I'd lost so much blood that the soil beneath his feet turned into a red slush."

As if crying, Forneus dropped his skull into his hands and caressed the top of his glass skull with his boney fingers.

"Thema, my lovely wife. My queen. Although she was pregnant, she fought against that Demon to free me. Stones, sticks, biting—she did all she could to get that monster off me. But in the end, it wasn't enough. As I lay on the ground, drained of blood, the Demon grabbed Thema and . . ."

Forneus's voice trailed away, and everything grew quiet. After a few seconds, Forneus continued.

"He ripped our unborn child from my Thema's belly, cut her throat, and tossed her body into the falls."

Suddenly Forneus made a fist and slammed it angrily against the ground, shaking the building. The snakes inside his chest started moving again, and Forneus raised his head to look at Arlo.

"But he wasn't finished. As my son lay on the ground, cold and bloody, crying for his mother, the Demon took his liberties with me."

"Liberties? You mean . . ."

"Yes. After beating me until I was incapacitated, the Demon raped me for hours while my son witnessed the atrocity."

"Gosh!"

"The thing no one tells you about Hell is that they want to strip you of everything. My wife, my son, my health, and my manhood—that creature took everything he could until I was nothing. Later that night, half dead and mourning my wife and child, another visitor came calling, a man named Dressler. His appearance made me lower my guard—he was a frail old man with a hump on his back, moving through the night, carrying a large bag. We sat down underneath the moon and began talking. Eventually, he presented himself as an Angel from Heaven. I don't know what it was. Maybe I was weak, or maybe I just wanted comfort after taking the beating from the Demon. But I easily accepted his words as truth. How he spoke, that steady soft voice comforted me. It made me drop my guard. Eventually, I told him everything. After hearing my story, Dressler took pity on me. As I sat crying about my losses, he, too, cried. I didn't understand how, but I felt close to him. Before the night's end, he promised to help me retrieve my wife and son from death."

"That was nice."

"But it was conditional—I had to become a guide for other lost souls wronged by Hell."

"Well . . . I would've done it."

"And so I did."

Arlo looked at the worms and snakes on Forneus's body, and his skin started crawling again.

"What do those things do?" he asked, pointing at Forneus's chest.

Forneus ran his fingers across his glass-enclosed chest. *"That night, the Angel put these creatures in my head and chest. 'The serpents will replenish your health and prevent you from aging until you rejoin your wife.' That is what he told me. He showed me how to use the snakes in my mission. The worms grant me the power to take the form of anything I choose. I was such a fool, and I believed him."*

"You mean like taking over another person's body?"

"Yes. It is how I entered the body of the boar. But there are other powers that the serpents possess that I don't completely understand."

"And that is how you raised me?"

"Yes. I brought you back from death by possessing Isadora."

"Why?"

"That is a tale for another time."

Arlo looked into the coins covering Forneus's eyes. He could tell there was something the creature was hiding from him. Arlo didn't want to pressure him, so he kept quiet.

"The Angel taught me how to raise the dead and guide them to the Black Fields, where lost souls were supposed to enter the Great Slumber. For hundreds of years, I resurrected millions, working endless days and nights in hopes of seeing my wife and child. And then I discovered another truth."

Captivated by Forneus's story, Arlo listened intently. *"What did you learn?"*

"I learned that the Demons of Hell are eternal liars."

Forneus lifted himself from the ground and banged his head again on the ceiling. This time he crouched down before he took his first step and walked over to Arlo. Slowly, he sat in front of Arlo with bones grinding and cracking.

"It turns out that the first and second visitors were the same Demon. That bastard murdered my family and returned to enslave me."

"How did you find out?"

"A third visitor. One night, while I was digging up a grave, one of Heaven's true Angels appeared in the graveyard. She told me that the Demon lied to me and that there would be no reunion with my wife and son—Thema is in Heaven, but my son . . ."

"Where is he?"

"My son is in Hell with the Demon that killed my wife—he's raising him as his own."

"Gosh!"

"I asked the Angel if she could help me get my son back, but she said God was angry, and there was no way he was willing to intercede on my behalf. All those dead souls I awakened were good souls without the blemish of sin; Hell handpicked them and, like an idiot, I resurrected those souls and gave them to the Demon. The Black Fields wasn't a place to enter the Great Slumber, but instead was one of four entrances into the domain of Hell. The Demon tricked me into sending millions of innocent souls to Hell, where they all suffer today."

"Wow."

"Yes. That Demon son of a bitch got the best of me. Heaven's punishment for me is an eternal life of atonement. I can't be with my wife until I repay the debt. And my son? Who knows if I'll ever see him? I don't know what he looks like, or even his name. I have no idea what kind of childhood he's experienced or what kind of man he's become. If I meet him by chance, his soul will be so corrupted by what he's learned that he'll try to take my soul to Hell for their tortuous pleasure."

"There's always a chance that your son's love for you will be greater than—"

Forneus slammed his fist on the ground again in anger. *"Shut up! You speak of a driveling hope that doesn't exist. Hell has him! They know I've stopped supplying the Black Fields with fresh innocents, and soon my son will come to drag me to Hell."*

Arlo sensed Forneus's anger rising and tried to change the subject. *"So Hell put those things in you?"*

Forneus rubbed his head with his hand. *"While they provide specific helpful abilities, their primary job is to torture me with their never-ending screams. The snakes? They're forever locked inside by a spell, and I descend to Hell forever if I somehow decipher the sorcery and free the serpents."*

Arlo was confused. *"Wait. You said you are here to suffer an eternal life of atonement. What does that mean?"*

"Each soul has an earthly value of one hundred years."

"And?"

"And I sent millions to Hell. You do the math."

"Whoa!"

"That's right. At a minimum, I'll be here for a billion years."

Arlo shook his head. *"Is there any way to shorten your sentence?"*

"For every good deed that saves a soul, Heaven will give me a reduction of fifty years."

Suddenly a blood-covered Isadora appeared at the entrance of the building, holding a dead fox in her arms. Her eyes had a bluish glow, making her seem even more frightening as the light from her eyes accentuated her half-decomposed face. She walked over to Arlo and dropped the carcass in front of him.

"You're probably hungry, so I brought you something to eat," she said in Arlo's head.

Arlo could only pretend he wasn't hungry for a few moments before jumping on the dead animal and biting into its skull. He peeled back the bone, slamming his face into the animal's brain. A deep, satisfying moan escaped his throat as he swallowed, savoring the raw meat. Meanwhile, Isadora sat down beside Forneus and watched Arlo consume his meal.

After eating the animal's brain, Arlo stuck his fingers underneath the fox's ribcage and pulled it apart like a giant clam shell. He didn't hesitate when he saw the animal's heart. Arlo reached in, yanked it free, and thrust it into his mouth so hard that his teeth peeled the skin off his hand.

When Arlo finished eating, he looked up from his meal and saw Isadora and Forneus watching him. The two were a spectacle sitting against the wall, like creatures from different worlds—Forneus, a towering skeleton of ancient bones lighting the room with the glow from his skull of worms, and Isadora, a tiny, disfigured corpse with luminous eyes. Although Arlo knew he was part of the death scene, seeing the two tortured souls was a dreadful fright and still terrified him. Feeling afraid and somewhat embarrassed, Arlo pushed the scraps of the animal away and sat against the wall.

"I-I'm ssssorry," his garbled voice spoke.

“’Tis ok-k-kay,” replied Isadora, struggling to speak while air rushed out of the hole in her face.

“Why do you continue to try to speak with your regular voice?” asked Isadora inside Arlo’s mind. *“Speaking in your head is much easier—and clearer.”*

Arlo tried shrugging, but his attempt was lost in his inability to control his body movements, making his shrug seem like a convulsion.

“I don’t know. I guess I haven’t gotten used to it yet. Maybe a part of me wants my old life back.”

Forneus shook his enormous head in disapproval and stood up. Crouching, he walked over to the remains of the dead fox and pushed his massive skeletal hand inside the creature’s chest. The leg of the animal jerked once, then again before raising itself from the floor to stand. With the hole in its head and its brain missing, it glared at Forneus with shimmering catlike eyes, growling and moaning, before finally sprinting out into the dark forest. As soon as the fox was gone, Forneus turned to face Arlo and Isadora.

“The two of you had better accept reality. You’re dead, and that’s the end of it. There’s no going back. You only have two choices—this zombie existence or the Deep Slumber, that’s it. Take this time to learn about your capabilities and ensure your loved ones are okay. But the existence you have is . . .”

Bewildered, Arlo suddenly stood. *“I completely forgot! Mom! Dad!”*

Stumbling and struggling to maintain his balance, Arlo ran out of the building into the forest, with Isadora running close behind.

7

The Army of Hell

As John laid on the bloody table, waiting for his master to arrive, he looked around the room and felt a sense of pride; the human intestines hanging from the ceiling and walls were just as he instructed—packed with blood and feces, filling the room with the wondrous stench of suffering. A small chunk of waste fell from the ceiling and landed on John's forehead, but he didn't object. The feces warmed his whole body, and he wiped the glorious mess all over his face.

"Balam will be satisfied," he whispered.

Suddenly all the intestines in the room started glowing like burning coals, casting a red light on John's naked body. Soon, the air was thick with the smell of sulfur.

"My Lord approaches," said John.

Suddenly there was a humming sound followed by moans and screams. John looked at the floor and saw the corpses thrashing around like they were alive. The decapitated head of one of the nurses suddenly opened her eyes.

"Noooo!" she screamed. "Get me out of here! He's coming to get me!"

The nurse's eyes started bleeding, and her tongue swelled into a thick purple chunk of meat, making her gag. The other bodies, missing their hearts and intestines, all reacted the same, and the room filled with cries of terror. The cries all reached a crescendo of suffering, and the room fell silent again.

"I am here," a deep voice boomed.

"Yes, my Lord," whispered John with his eyes closed. "I am your willing servant."

"Are you prepared to see your master?"

"I am."

All the intestines in the room began to swell, filling with fluid and emitting a foul odor much more potent than before. Suddenly they exploded, sending their contents shooting throughout the room. As the liquid splashed everywhere, John closed his eyes and prepared himself.

"Will you pay the fee?"

"I will."

Suddenly with one loud ripping sound, all the skin on John's body tore off.

"AAAAARRRRRGGG!" screamed John, trying to take the pain.

A black mist appeared at the bottom of the bed in the shape of a towering, voluptuous woman. John lifted his head to look at the shadow and regretted it immediately—his eyes began burning, and large puss-filled sores appeared on his eyelids. John laid his bloody, hairless head on the table and closed his eyes.

"Please forgive my curiosity, Lord. I meant no disrespect."

The smoke slowly melted away, and a tall woman dressed in a hooded black robe appeared at the foot of John's bed. Balam's coarse red skin was scaly, resembling the skin of a snake, and it constantly moved, sliding along her bones like silk, making her appearance grotesque. She stared at John with two enormous, mirrored eyes that were so close to one another that they appeared to be one.

As John twisted in agony, Balam extended one of her long fingers and touched John's skinless foot, causing his leg to burst into flame.

"AAAAARRRRRGGG!" John screamed again.

"Hehehehe," Balam laughed, her demonic voice deep like a man's. "Do you hate us?"

"I d-d-don't," replied John.

The fire on his foot went out, and Balam moved to John's side. She waved her hand over his face, and the sores on John's eyes lids disappeared.

"You may open your eyes."

John opened his eyes and saw Balam standing over him.

"I see you have taken another soul."

Trying not to let the pain affect his words, John replied. "Yes, Lord. I took the soul of the boy Manuel."

Balam closed her eyes and breathed deeply. "Goooood. I can feel the energy of the others inside you. They make you strong."

John smiled and let his eyes fall to the floor. He was happy his actions pleased his master.

"The time to cover the world in darkness is upon us, and now is the time to construct Hell's soldiers."

John wanted to ask questions, but he wasn't sure how to speak to the Demon. Balam saw the confused look on John's face and reached out to touch his blistering scalp. As soon as her fingertip touched John, hundreds of plump maggots with metallic teeth burst from his head and started feeding on his flesh. Unable to ignore his pain, John began trembling while Balam turned away.

"If you do not dare to ask the simplest questions, how can you be trusted to lead such a powerful army?" she snapped.

Unable to wait on the mercy of Balam to take the feasting creatures away, John raised himself on the table and used his hands to wipe the worms from his head, peeling chunks of his scalp with them.

"I'm sorry, Lord. I will do better," whispered John, trying his best to fight through the stinging sensation on his scalp.

Balam turned back to face John. "You will use the children's bodies as carriers of this." Balam opened her palm to reveal a tiny red vile.

John moved close to Balam's hand. "What is it?"

"This vile contains the seedlings of Huturo, a creature of joyous pain from the mud on the banks of the river Styx."

John took the vile into his palm and stared at it.

"Once this pathogen attaches itself to the child, it will corrupt the parents, transforming them into Huturo mud creatures."

"What will it do to the children?"

"Nothing. We need those souls to build the fortresses of Hell. But their parents? They'll become Huturo, willing to fight to the death. We will use the Huturo to cleanse this world of the annoying humans before the final battle."

"The fight against Heaven?"

"Obviously."

John shook the vile and looked at it again. "How do I deliver it?"

"Bring in one of the youth."

John blinked, and there was a knock at the door. The door opened, and a thin boy dressed in a hospital gown walked in. As soon as the child saw Balam, his skin ripped from his body. The child immediately fell to the floor, screaming. As the skinless child lay squirming on the floor, Balam walked over to him and dropped the vile into his open mouth. The Demon waved his hand over the child, and the child's jaw cracked, opening and repeatedly closing until the glass container was gone. Blood poured from his mouth, and the bloody child raised himself from the floor and ran out of the room. Balam turned to face John.

"It is done. The virus is replicating to all the children beyond this door."

John looked down at the floor. "Is that all that is needed?"

"The Huturo will cover the land very quickly. It is your job to ensure each soldier is strong and their transformation is permanent."

"How will I do this, my Lord?"

"The old Witch Asura has been your servant since the beginning of your four earthly births. Use her dark powers to protect your army. The Huturo are weak after their transformation, and if you do not find a way to protect them during their fragile state, they will revert to their human forms."

John's eyes widened. "There will be thousands of Huturo."

"Wrong—there will be millions in only a short period. You will need to devise a method of delivery."

John looked worried. "But what if I can't find a way to deliver the elixir?"

"Then you will receive a punishment worse than any pain you've ever experienced. Here, let me give you a taste."

Balam waved her hand, and John rose in the air.

"My Lord! I believe you! I beg for your mercy!" pleaded John.

Balam smiled and waved her hand again.

"Ah, but this pain is necessary for your understanding. Failure is not an option."

A tiny hole appeared in John's chest just above his heart. There was a loud thump, and John winced in agony as his heart exited his chest, blood splattering onto Balam's face. As John watched his heart beating outside his body, he felt something pulling his back into the hole in his chest.

"AAAAAHHH! NOOOOO!" screamed John.

Soon, half his back was through the opening, cracking his ribs and pulling on muscles he never knew existed. John had never known such a level of excruciating agony, and his twisted facial expressions registered as much. He could feel the center of his spine folding in half, inching through the tiny hole in his body as slowly as possible for maximum impact on every nerve. John realized that Balam wanted him to understand what awaited on the other side of failure, to make him know that doing so was not an option. The torture of feeling every part of his existence pulled through the hole in his chest not only numbed his arms and legs, it deadened his acceptance of defeat.

After trying to ignore the pain, the tortuous experience became too much for John to bear.

"I understand, Lord. I will not fail you," John said.

Just as he was about to black out, John understood how Balam was punishing him—by turning his body inside out.

Suddenly there was a flash of light, and John fell to the floor. As he lay gasping for air, Balam stood over him, smiling.

"This is but a taste of what awaits your failure."

John touched his chest and was grateful that the hole was gone. He sloshed in the blood and entrails until he climbed to his knees beneath Balam.

"I will not fail you, my Lord."

Balam walked to the nearest wall containing human intestines and extended her hand. Suddenly the intestines started throbbing, and thick black veins appeared in the flesh. A tiny bubble appeared at the ends of the intestines that quickly grew larger until small infant human heads appeared. Soon the babies were crying, thrashing about on the tail end of the intestines, like hungry animals. Balam extended her hand, and the monsters fell from the wall, slithered across the floor, shot underneath her robe, and started eating her flesh.

"Do not fail us," said Balam while she closed her eyes. Suddenly her robe fell, and she was gone.

8

Arlo's Parents

Claire sat on the back porch with a blanket wrapped around her shoulders, staring out into the forest. After looking out into the snow-covered trees for a few moments, she quickly grabbed the telephone receiver from the table and placed it to her ear—there was only the dial tone. Claire hung up and immediately grabbed her cell phone. When she didn't see any new messages or missed calls, Claire slammed the phone on the table in frustration.

"Arlo, where the hell are you?" she whispered.

Suddenly the backdoor opened behind her, and her husband walked out. Jamie looked at his wife's face and sighed, flopping down in the chair beside her.

"Babe, it's late. When are you coming to bed? You know I have to work tomorrow."

Ignoring him, Claire grabbed the flashlight from the table and shined it out into the backyard.

"I'm not sleeping yet. I need to be awake in case Arlo calls."

Jamie shoved his fists into his jeans, stretched his legs, and banged his feet together until icy mud fell off his sneakers.

"The weatherman is saying we're getting more snow tonight. I need to take that bag of ice melt out of the garage and spread it on the driveway before the snow gets here. Do you want to give me a hand with it?"

Claire picked up the phone and rechecked the dial tone. "No, Jamie. I need to stay by the phone."

"There's no need to worry. Arlo probably just went out to blow off some steam."

Claire looked at her husband in disbelief. "Blow off some steam?! For a whole two weeks?!"

Jamie shook his head and looked away in frustration. "Let the cops do their jobs. They've only been searching for a couple of days."

Claire's eyes filled with tears. "But it's not like Arlo to disappear like this," she complained.

Jamie belched and smacked his stomach. "One thing's for sure. When that boy makes it back, we've got to have a man-to-man talk about responsibility."

Claire's mouth fell open. "Really, Jamie? Our son has been missing for two weeks, and you're thinking about hitting him? Really?"

"I didn't mean it like that. I'm just saying . . ."

"Oh, just shut up! I know good and damned well what you meant!"

Jamie stood up and walked to the edge of the porch. "So what if I was talking about disciplining him? You baby that boy at every turn. If you're not making his food just as he likes or walking up to his room to give him a goodnight kiss, you're propping up his feelings with that stupid poetry book. I don't know how to tell you this, but a boy his age is supposed to be out partying and banging girls. You have him staying in the house all the time, wrapped up in his emotions like some goddamned girl. No wonder he's missing. He's probably confused as hell!"

Claire grabbed the flashlight and stomped down the stairs into the backyard. She could hear Jamie calling after her, but she ignored him.

"Arlo probably ran away to get the hell away from you, asshole," she whispered.

With the blanket wrapped around her shoulders, Claire kept walking until she reached the yard's edge. Soon she realized walking too far would be a mistake—she didn't bring the phones, and she wouldn't hear the phone ringing if there were news about Arlo. Still, Claire didn't have the energy to fight with Jamie; he could be a real bully regarding their son. She thought Jamie would grow to regret his behaviors with Arlo, especially after the police found the body of Arlo's best friend's father a few houses up from theirs. But instead of regretfully analyzing his shortcomings in fathering, Jamie took that tragedy as an opportunity to insult the deceased man's memory by assigning blame to his son for Arlo's disappearance.

Suddenly the door creaked open, and Claire turned to see Jamie walk into the house.

"Prick," she mumbled as she walked back to the porch. She'd only taken a few steps when she remembered the pack of cigarettes in her pocket. She stopped in the middle of the yard, took out the box, and popped one in her mouth.

"Shit!" Claire cursed, realizing she'd left her lighter in the house. She snatched the cigarette from her lips, crumpled it, and tossed it on the ground.

"Oh, well. Arlo would be pissed if he knew I started smoking again."

Suddenly the memory of Arlo's smile came rushing back, and Claire couldn't hold in her sadness. She lifted part of the blanket, buried her face, and sobbed deeply. Arlo was Claire's best friend, and she'd never told him how much their bond meant. Claire's mother was a strict disciplinarian and it instilled a level of coldness in her that was sometimes difficult to detect. Claire remembered one moment between her and Arlo that now stood out like a sore thumb; she remembered how Arlo had come to show her a poem he'd written about their friendship. As he handed it to her, the emotion in his eyes lit his face with pride. But Claire was preoccupied with something on TV, and merely glanced at the poem before returning her attention to her favorite TV show.

"That's nice, baby. Did you finish your homework?"

At the time, Arlo took it in stride and returned to his room. But now that he was gone, Claire couldn't stop thinking about the pain in her son's eyes that day. Knowing that she hurt him cut deeper than the sharpest blade.

As tears poured down Claire's face, she remembered how she'd made his gift of love seem so tiny and trivial. But now Claire could see how misguided her actions had been. Arlo's soul was soft and unique, a rarity amongst the field of thorns sharpened by chauvinism. Sometimes words mattered more than actions, and Claire should've recognized Arlo's sensitivity. Claire would give anything to hear his voice now. But no matter how hard Claire tried, her son was missing, and she, his mother, was standing alone in the darkness with nothing but tears and memories. The silence in her suffering was louder than anything she'd ever experienced. Jamie couldn't understand because he wasn't as close to Arlo as Claire.

Claire heard rustling behind her, and she quickly turned to face the dark forest.

"Who's there?" she asked, pointing the flashlight into the forest.

Claire hit the button, but the light flickered off and on. After slapping the plastic contraption with her palm, the light finally lit up, and Claire shined it into the trees. She immediately saw the silhouettes of a boy and a girl standing side by side in the forest. Seeing the shadows took her breath away, and Claire dropped the flashlight on the ground. She picked up the light again, but the light wouldn't turn on this time.

"Shit!" she cursed, banging on the flashlight.

Claire looked up and saw the silhouettes inching through the trees toward her. She knew she should run, but her feet wouldn't listen to her brain, so she remained frozen. As the figures moved closer, Claire became mesmerized by the strides of the two shadows—different yet similar. Their half-drunken, off-balance dance reminded her of Jamie when he'd had one too many drinks.

Suddenly the two figures stopped walking and stood swaying.

"Uhhhhhhh," a voice moaned from the shadows.

Claire dropped the flashlight and covered her mouth.

"J-Jamie!" she stuttered. "H-help!"

Suddenly everything fell silent, and Claire stood trapped, unable to move while the two figures stared at her. There was a break in the clouds, and the yellow moon appeared, casting an eerie golden light on the frozen forest. Slowly, the shadows melted away and revealed the two people standing in the snowy woods.

"AAAAAAHHHH!" she screamed.

A teenage boy and girl stood before Claire, both nightmarish in appearance and drenched in blood. Their faces were masks of terror: the girl's left cheek was missing chunks of flesh, her jaw displayed decaying muscles, and thick, green drool oozed from the hole in her face; the boy wasn't missing pieces of his face but had numerous purple spider veins spreading from his chin to up to his dead white eye. Both had enormous holes in their chests.

Claire tried to scream again, but the smell of decaying flesh entered her open mouth, suffocating her ability to talk. Feeling weak, Claire took an uneasy step away from the zombies. As she attempted to take a second step, the boy extended his arms.

"Mooommm," he groaned.

Claire's heart was pounding, and she started crying. She looked around frantically for a way to escape the zombies, but the world turned small inside her fear. The stench of death was everywhere.

"This can't be happening!" she whispered.

The zombie children continued moving toward Claire with outstretched arms, their gray, shoeless feet dragging across the frozen grass like pieces of meat.

"Aaaaaaaahhhh," the boy groaned again, his one white eye fixed on his target.

Claire was shivering uncontrollably now. With each approaching step the zombies took, the air grew thinner, more frigid, and more challenging to take into her lungs—her mouth became a narrow straw that couldn't take in enough oxygen.

Suddenly the clouds took pity on Claire and swallowed the moon and, along with it, the invaders' faces. As if someone from the heavens heard her cries of terror, the clouds laid a blanket of shadow on everything, hiding the hideous death creeping toward her through the night.

Grateful for cover, Claire turned around to run away. But she remembered what she saw and tripped, crashing to the ground clumsily.

"No!" said Claire, feeling like a character in one of those dumb horror movies where the person fell, trying to escape. She tried climbing to her feet by placing her palms on the icy grass and lifting herself quickly, but she underestimated how slippery the ground was, and the ice pushed her arms apart, and she almost fell on her face.

"Waaait," the girl zombie whispered with disgusting green bubbles forming on her face.

"No! Get away from me!" screamed Claire.

The two zombies were now standing over her. Dark or not, Claire could see all their terrifying features—the organs inside their open chest cavities, black and frozen like freezer-burned meat; the flesh of other victims was in their teeth, and their decomposing skin looked shiny like wax.

Claire was sobbing heavily now. It was time for her to die; all she had left was to lie down and try to squeeze the reality of her demise out like an old dishrag. She closed her eyes, just as she'd done as a child when she was afraid of the dark, curled up in a fetal position, and waited for the two children from Hell to take her away. It was no point fighting anymore. They would take what was theirs and leave her bones to ice over in the forest.

"Mooooom," the boy moaned once more.

The hair on the back of Claire's neck stood up. She recognized something in the boy's voice, a familiarity wrapped in the macabre that penetrated her fear. Claire began asking herself questions she couldn't finish. She didn't want to open her eyes because she was afraid; the truth was in front of her, and she only needed to seek visual confirmation.

Was it him? Could it be? Impossible.

A metallic sound arose behind her, interrupting Claire's thoughts, and she quickly opened her eyes. She turned to see her husband Jamie standing a few feet away with his rifle aimed at the two monsters.

"Jamie! No!" screamed Claire.

But it was too late. Jamie pulled the trigger hitting the boy squarely in the chest, spraying his black blood everywhere and sending him flying back into the bushes. The girl, furious at the damage done to the zombie boy, released a terrifying growl. With glowing red eyes, she rushed toward Jamie, but before getting close, he fired again. This time he missed his target and shredded a tree beside the zombie girl, stopping her in her tracks. As Jamie searched his pockets for more ammunition, the girl ran to the boy lying in the bushes, lifted him to his feet, and took off running into the forest.

"Holy shit! What the fuck?" Jamie asked after reloading.

Claire climbed to her feet and ran into the forest. "Arlo! Baby, it's mommy!" she screamed.

Jamie looked at his wife in disbelief. "What?!"

Unable to find the zombie children, Claire turned and returned to her husband. "I think that thing was Arlo."

"But how is that possible? You saw it; no human being could walk around with their insides exposed like that."

Claire walked past her husband and into the house while Jamie stood holding the weapon, staring into the forest in disbelief. "Did I just shoot my son?" he whispered.

After a few minutes, Jamie walked back into the house and sat on the back porch, terrified at what he'd done.

9

It's Worse Than the First Time

The whole world was burning, and Arlo was in the center of it. As Isadora dragged him through the forest, Arlo could barely stand up—the gunshot wound from his father's weapon ignited Arlo's whole world, transforming the cold forest into a cauldron of fire; the zombie Sun Oil returned with a vengeance, burning Arlo worse than before. The ground was on fire, and everywhere he stepped caused the soles of his feet to sizzle like bacon.

Arlo looked up into the treetops and saw an owl looking down at him. As soon as the animal made eye contact with him, it burst into flame, hooting as the children ran underneath the tree. Finally, with its wings burning like a fiery phoenix, the bird took flight, raining down embers on the two as it flew away.

The teenagers stumbled down a hill into a ravine filled with icy water. But to Arlo, the water was a raging mini volcano, a pit filled with molten lava that blistered his genitals with every splash-filled step. He could feel the heat rising from beneath his feet, the rocks on the creek bed radiating like a raging fireplace.

They continued running along the edge of the stream and suddenly stopped—sitting on the edge of the creek with its face buried in the water was an enormous bear. The creature sensed it had company and turned to look at the two trespassers before it exploded into fire. Arlo saw the beast and rejoiced inside. Although the creature looked like a walking Fire Demon with icy blue fish inside its gut, it had a gigantic head filled with slushy, cooling brain matter. Just thinking about the soothing brains made Arlo weak in the knees. But Isadora made a right and moved in a different direction.

"Uhhhhhhh," Arlo moaned in protest. "Neeeeeed."

"No," replied Isadora's voice in Arlo's mind. *"He's too big, and he'll make the fires worse—he's not worth the fight."*

Isadora continued pulling Arlo through the forest, but Arlo was almost finished; his chest was burning so bad that it felt like melting wax. He coughed a couple of times and tasted dry, bitter ash in his mouth. Smoke was billowing from his nose and mouth like a locomotive, his eyelids crackling like kindling as his eyeballs grew hotter and hotter. Arlo tried speaking to Isadora with his mind, but his brain wouldn't function; all his thoughts were of the bullets that pierced his flesh, igniting his world and turning everything into flame.

The two suddenly stopped, and Isadora pointed through the trees to a small, dimly lit hunter's shack.

"There! Do you see it?"

"Uhhhhh . . ."

Suddenly an old man walked past the dirty window with an old metal coffee pot in his hand. It was all that Arlo needed to see. He exploded in a sprint to the hut, moving with a quickness he'd never before possessed. Like a madman, he ripped the door from its hinges. The old man turned, dropped the coffee pot, and looked at Arlo in surprise.

"Jesus Christ! What the . . ."

The man reached for his rifle leaning against the wall but didn't have ammunition. Before he could locate the shotgun shells, Arlo was on him. He grabbed the old man and bit his skull.

"AAAAHHHH!" the old man screamed.

He pushed Arlo away and fell to the floor, blood gushing from the teeth marks on his scalp. The man's eyes fell on a metal poker, and he dove for it as Arlo attempted to attack him again. Just as Arlo was about to land, the man extended the poker and stabbed the boy in his stomach. But Arlo was unfazed by the injury, and he grabbed the man's wrist and twisted it until it broke.

"AAAAAHHH! Dear God!" screamed the man.

Arlo grabbed the metal poker and repeatedly hit the man on his head. After three blows, he lost consciousness. Arlo bit into his skull again, but he couldn't open it because it was too hard for his teeth.

"BRAAAAINNNS," Arlo moaned.

Arlo jabbed the poker into the man's eye socket and pushed up, sending blood squirting all over his face. Slowly he pried off the top of the man's skull, exposing his brains. Arlo scooped a handful of the man's brains out and shoved them into his mouth. A deep freeze shot through his nerves, causing Arlo to fall back dazed—the brain matter was much sweeter than the animal brains and more potent in removing his pain. Within seconds, all the fire was gone, and the pain in Arlo's chest was a distant memory. Arlo lifted the man's head from the floor and slurped the remaining brain matter from his skull. A sense of calm swept over him, and he could think again.

Arlo continued licking the inside of the man's skull until the only thing that remained were the blood vessels attached to the bone. Finally, he stood up and looked at the mess he'd created.

"What have I done?" he asked inside his mind. *"I've murdered an innocent man."*

Arlo tore out of the cabin into the night to escape the man's corpse. He spotted Isadora waiting for him a few feet from the house and was about to run to her when he stopped. The sky above him was pounding with thunder. Arlo looked up and saw that the sky was clear. Yet the rumbling of the thunder grew louder, shaking the ground beneath his feet.

Suddenly a loud crack sounded, and dozens of lightning bolts shot from one side of the sky to the other, stretching out like long fingers of fire. But they didn't disappear. Instead, they sizzled the sky, lighting up everything beneath them.

"Isadora! What's happening?" Arlo asked, shrinking to his knees, staring up into the night sky.

But Isadora paid no attention to Arlo or the sky. She grabbed a raccoon from a bush, killed it, and started eating its brains.

The thunder in the sky grew louder and louder. Finally, a pencil-thin white lightning bolt shot from the sky and hit Arlo on the top of his head. The electricity illuminated his skull for a few seconds and caused light to shoot from his eyes.

"AAAHHHHH," Arlo screamed.

But his scream was not of pain; the lightning didn't hurt him. Instead, it moved inside his skull like a small laser until finally disappearing, taking the thunder and fire in the sky along with it.

After checking the sky, Arlo slowly climbed to his feet and stumbled over to Isadora.

"What the hell was that?" asked Arlo.

"What was what?" asked Isadora, preoccupied with her meal.

Arlo lifted his trembling arm and pointed to the sky.

"The lightning. You didn't see it?"

Isadora ripped out the raccoon's guts and tossed aside the carcass before stuffing them into her mouth.

"Oh, you mean Ayiba's Marker? No, I didn't see it. The sky was normal for me—it's like that for all the undead, I can't see yours, and you can't see mine. The lightning and thunder are for the sinner."

"Ayiba's Marker? What's that?"

"Tonight was the first time you killed a human. The first time the undead takes a human life, Heaven places a marker, the Ayiba, inside the skull of the offender."

"A marker? For what?"

"It's a way for Heaven to track us, to know how much evil we've committed. Think of the whole world as a GPS screen on a cellphone, and you're a red dot. Heaven engraved a tracking device inside your skull, and now it has a way to track where you go and who you kill."

"How do you know so much?"

"Forneus. That old bag of bones is chatty as fuck. When he found me, I thought he'd never shut up. He damned near talked my goddamned ear off my head."

"Yeah, he did talk a lot when I met him."

"But he's a good guy—kind of lonely, though. I'm just happy he was here to help me. He told you about the years he has to repay, right?"

"Yeah, one hundred years per person."

"That same rule applies to us. If you take a human life without justifiable cause, you'll have to repay those hundred years on Judgment Day."

"So that means . . ."

"Yep. After that feeding, you're indebted to that old bastard for one hundred years."

"Shit! One hundred years?! That seems unfair."

"It doesn't matter. It's hard to argue innocence with Heaven, you know? After all, they know everything about you since you were born. I guess they figure by the time you opened that man's skull, you knew the consequences."

Isadora nodded to the sky.

"They know you know right from wrong because they taught it to everyone. And worse, they won't say or do anything to stop you from fucking up. With those odds, Forneus says many of our kind can't hack it and search for ways to get out."

"Like suicide?"

Isadora started laughing, and her terrifying cackle cleared all the trees of sleeping birds. *"Suicide for the undead? That's funny as fuck!"*

Isadora reached inside her rib cage, attempting to scratch an itching organ, and her whole body shuddered. Feeling disgusted, Arlo quickly looked away.

"Our shelf lives are short in these decaying bodies—some of us let the fire take us away, while others allow people with powerful weapons to force us out. Either way, once we sleep and Judgment Day comes, we get judged for the lives we took."

Arlo looked up at the night sky. *"You mean to tell me God's watching?"*

"Forneus told me God doesn't watch, but his Angels are watching all the time. They're snitching on you as we speak."

"And you believe that?"

"That lightning show didn't convince you?"

Arlo thought about what Isadora said and turned away. He had been anxious to stop the fire but never considered whether his victim deserved to have his life extinguished. God had every right to punish him, and Arlo didn't have a worthy defense against what he'd done—murder was murder. It didn't matter that Arlo had been burning from the Sun Oil; who was he to decide to take a life? The man, indeed, had a family. What if he had children? A wife? There was so much pain under Arlo's half-baked decision that he trembled at the thought of it all.

After thinking about the years of suffering God had planned for him, Arlo turned to Isadora. *"Have you taken a life?"*

"Yeah, a few, but I can only remember the first two; there was this arrogant bitch back at school who I hated. I don't remember how but I stumbled on her after she finished cheerleading practice one night. My second was this crippled old lady I took pity on. Dying was better than living for that old bag. She had a hump in her back and her fingers were curled with arthritis. Trust me. I did her a favor."

Arlo looked at Isadora in disbelief—her words were so cavalier and devoid of humanity. To Arlo, Isadora spoke of the stamping out of her victims like she was describing a place she'd visited, or a TV show. Isadora was truly becoming a monster, and Arlo hoped taking his victim's life wouldn't put the same ice in his veins.

Isadora looked at the horizon. *"Hey, we'd better get back. The sun's coming up. It's harder to fend for yourself when people can see you. Besides, you haven't had the important talk with Forneus yet."*

"Important talk? About what?"

"Forneus can tell you better than I can. Let's get out of here."

10

Gathering Storms

"Okay, John. You can remove the blanket now."

John threw aside the blanket and sat up on the bed. He ran his fingers along his skin and smiled, happy to see his skin healed.

"Your work is exemplary, Asura."

The old woman smiled and passed a stack of clothing to John. "I live for your praise."

John climbed off the bed and got dressed. When he finished, he turned to Asura. "You and I have been together for many years."

"This is true, Lord."

"Although my spirit wears the souls of multiple people inside this body, we all draw from the same pool of memories."

Asura smiled. "My Lord wishes to know about the Witches of Blood Mountain."

"Many years ago, I heard of a trio of Witches living close to our forest home."

"Yes, John. The Witches lived close to your home, and one even took care of you when your mortal mother fell ill."

John smiled. "So they do exist."

"Most certainly, Lord."

"Where are they now?"

Asura's eyes sparkled, and she flashed a sinister smile.

"They still live together on Blood Mountain."

"Would they come if you called them?"

"The Witches have never left their home."

"That is not the question I asked, Asura."

Asura started giggling and tried to cover her rotten-toothed smile. "One day, the sisters cursed me as an ugly abomination unsuitable for a husband. I took my revenge by chopping off the right hand of the youngest and most beautiful sister, Rita. For years, I've kept her hand in a jar filled with widow poison, protected by a spell to repel or kill any man seeking her hand in marriage. To this day, I have never tried to bend her to my will, but if I do, Rita will come—and so will her sisters."

"Good. Balam has spoken. The next phase of our plan begins. Gather the Witches of Blood Mountain and bring them here."

"Yes, John."

John opened the door of the operating room and walked out with Asura. Two small visitors immediately greeted him by touching his arm.

"The Gatekeepers," John whispered, greeting them with a smile.

He recognized the children. They were the kids he touched when he arrived at the hospital. But the children were drastically different now. Their appearances were hideous; their faces hung off their skulls like they were made of rubber, stretching so far down that they touched the floor. Each had a small black horn protruding from what was supposed to be their forehead.

John turned to the first monster child. "The two of you will go upstairs and position yourselves on the rooftop. If someone trespasses, you know what to do."

As soon as the children limped away, John walked through the hallway, Asura following closely behind. John marveled at how many kids he'd reached; there were children crowded together on the floor, lined against the walls, and crammed into adjoining patient rooms, peering out into the hallway at him as he walked by. John walked through the crowd and exited the front door.

Standing on top of the stairs, John surveyed his audience; a thousand children stood in front of the hospital, all silent and waiting for their master's instructions. Some children were barely old enough to walk, while others were teenagers carrying babies in their arms. But they were all there at John's request.

John's eyes fell on the pile of adult bodies lying on the ground in the center of the crowd.

"What is this?" John asked, motioning to the corpses.

"Those are the bodies of a few protesting parents and local constables; they arrived before you met with our Dark Lord Balam," replied Asura.

John went down the stairs, and the crowd of children separated. He walked up to the pile of dead bodies and breathed deeply—the mixture of decomposing bodies and urine, along with the buzz of hungry flies, was an intoxicating scene that he thoroughly enjoyed.

"What a waste. I would've liked to see the disbelievers transformed by the seedlings of Huturo."

"We are all anxious to see our glorious soldiers, Lord."

John turned to face Asura. "How would you like to go out for an inspection?"

A look of worry appeared on Asura's wrinkled face. "Are you sure that's a good idea, John? You are most safe here."

"Balam will not allow failure, and I must be sure the seedlings of Huturo are working. Don't worry, Asura. I will visit a familiar area of my upbringing to avoid surprises."

Asura flashed a worried look at John, and he smiled.

"Don't worry, Asura. You will travel with me as my protection. Cheer up. I'm going to visit my mom."

11

Running Out of Reality

Arlo sat on the floor, watching Isadora lap at the blood on her hands like a dog. He was surprised at how easily she made peace with her existence. Everything moved around her like water flowing over a rock in a creek; she seemed to accept her place in a world of death and said nothing to indicate otherwise. The damp, rotting world around her didn't wear on her soul as it did Arlo's.

After watching Isadora for several moments, Arlo inspected himself; the skin on his hands had numerous dark bruises and was wrinkled like he'd soaked them in water. His appearance was worsening, and there was nothing he could do to stop it.

Arlo looked down and spotted a hole in his pant leg. He inserted two fingers into the fabric and pulled, ripping the cloth, making the hole larger. When he saw his thigh, Arlo became dismayed.

"Shit," he thought.

His legs were more bruised than his hands, and the skin was peeling off his thigh like a snake's skin. Arlo moved his leg to inspect the injury further, and a disgusting odor rose from beneath him. He could smell his genitals rotting; the stench was a stark reminder of his previous life, warm and soothing, filled with the comfort of things he'd taken for granted. Arlo remembered all the times his mother had asked him to shower and how he'd barked in protest. Arlo didn't realize those moments were gifts. Now the thought of the fresh, clean liquid splashing on his decaying body felt like a sin, something Arlo didn't deserve.

Frustrated, Arlo shook his head in disgust. *"I can't believe that son of a bitch shot me,"* he complained with his inner voice.

Isadora looked at Arlo and sighed. *"I know your emotions are all over the place, but at least you got to see them again."*

"I'm a little depressed, but I'm mostly pissed off. Why would my dad shoot me?"

Arlo ran his hand across the numerous holes on his chest before inserting his index finger into one of the larger holes; when he removed his finger, there was black fluid on it.

"I tried to warn you, but you ran out of here before I could stop you. Returning to your family is risky because they might see you and won't understand what you've become. To them, you're a monster, something from a nightmare."

Arlo felt the ground vibrating, and he looked around. A spark flashed in the far corner of the room, and slowly a dim golden light appeared, illuminating a giant skeleton.

"Ahhhh," sighed Forneus. *"No matter how much I rest, these old painful bones torment me."*

Bones cracking, Forneus rose from the floor and walked across the room, his crown of worms and chest of serpents igniting his path. He sat down in front of the two teens with a thunderous clang, his ancient bones kicking up a small cloud of dust in front of them.

"Aren't you hungry?" asked Isadora. *"I can get something from the forest if you'd like."*

Forneus ignored Isadora's question and turned to Arlo. *"Your parents saw you?"*

"Yes."

"I've pulled millions of bodies from the earth and delivered the same warning but none listened. As soon as they emerge from the grave, they all run to their families, searching for their previous lives. Indeed, the family bond is one of the strongest connections in the universe. Unfortunately,

your parents saw you in your current state of decomposition. That can be difficult for anyone to accept, but trust me, it helps your family more than it hurts. Now they know you're dead, and subconsciously they realize you've become something that cannot exist in their world."

Arlo became angry at Forneus's words and slammed his fist on the floor. *"Why did you do this to me? Why not let me stay dead?"* asked Arlo.

The worms in Forneus's head began sizzling, screaming louder as he glared at Arlo through metallic eyes. *"Careful, boy. I do not tolerate disrespect,"* growled Forneus.

But Arlo couldn't contain his anger. *"You think I deserve this shit? Look at me! I was better off dead beneath that house in the forest. Now I'm here killing people and eating their brains like an animal! I don't deserve this, and neither does Isadora!"*

Forneus stood, stomped past Arlo to the other side of the room, and sat down on the ground. He stared at Arlo as the snakes inside his chest became a furious mess, twisting and wrapping themselves around one another, igniting a blue flame that enveloped Forneus's body. Eventually, the fire died, and the giant skeleton lowered his head and fell silent.

Isadora jumped up from the floor. *"Are you crazy? Why did you speak to him like that?"*

Furious, Arlo tried speaking, but only a dry moan escaped his throat. He quickly adjusted and began yelling at Isadora through his thoughts.

"He deserves it! Forneus had no right to bring us back from the dead! No fucking right at all!"

Isadora stood in front of Arlo. *"I don't know if you realize it, but Forneus has been a gift to us! He helped me deal with the fact that John exploited me and tricked me into sending my parents to their deaths. He allowed you to see your family one last time, and he did all this while suffering for his wife and son. Doesn't that entitle him to a little respect?"*

"Stop making him out to be some tortured Angel. Forneus is a selfish prick with an agenda. I mean, why did he bring us here? Why aren't we in Heaven?"

"He told me the reason! You're the only person too damned caught up in self-pity to listen to what he has to say!"

"Well, he hasn't told me shit! And his tortured soul routine is getting old!"

Arlo walked past Forneus's bones to the entrance. Just as he was about to exit, Isadora called out to him. *"Arlo!"*

"What?"

"I know this thought hasn't crossed your mind, but there are others like us."

Arlo shrugged. *"So what?"*

"Maybe you should appreciate that you and I have someone to teach us. Trust me, others struggled alone, and Forneus is at the top of that list. Who knows how long he's been without anyone to talk to?"

"Whatever."

Isadora turned away from Arlo. *"Although we look nothing like the people we were, I'm happy you're here with me, and I'm not alone."*

Isadora's words startled Arlo, and he looked back at the decaying monster standing in the shadows. There was humanity in Isadora, and this was the first time he could see it.

Arlo walked out of the building and looked up into the sky. *"The sun is setting. I guess I'd better find something to eat,"* Arlo said. He could feel the heat in his body rising, and he wanted to stop it before it became unbearable.

Arlo stumbled through the forest, looking for an easy kill that wouldn't require him to exert too much energy. He spotted two squirrels at the base of a tree, but his staggering alerted the creatures, and they scampered away before he could reach them. Arlo continued his search for dinner but saw nothing worth pursuing, so he pushed deeper into the forest.

Soon the forest was pitch black, and Arlo became frustrated; he was far from the building and still hadn't found food. As he continued walking, Arlo felt a burning sensation inside his chest.

"I need to eat something fast," he whispered.

Arlo made a turn by a large tree and started running. Soon he heard the trickling of water and stopped. After listening for a few moments, Arlo picked up on the stream's location and pushed through a set of bushes. When he emerged, he froze—standing in the center of the stream was an enormous black bear with its back to Arlo. It was slapping the water with its paws, trying to catch fish. Arlo knew taking advantage of the creature would be difficult because it towered over Arlo and seemed like it could quickly dispatch him.

"I have to surprise him," said Arlo inside his mind, trying to convince himself that he could take the creature. The heat inside Arlo's body was much hotter now, and soon he would be out of options.

Arlo searched the grass for the most silent path to the creek's edge. After locating it, he ran out of the bushes. The creature turned around before Arlo could reach him, and reared its hind legs to face its attacker, freezing Arlo in his tracks. But what scared Arlo most was the bear's eyes: bright yellow flames burning inside its colossal eye sockets, making the bear seem like a creature from Hell.

"Uhhhhh," Arlo's voice cried as he attempted to scream. He turned around to run back into the forest but landed on his stomach. In a second, the bear was on him.

"Do you respect me now?" blared a deep voice in Arlo's head. *"Answer me, you ungrateful child!"*

The bear slashed Arlo's back with its sharp claws and walked around in a circle, stalking the boy like prey.

"If you crave the Great Sleep, I will send you there!"

Arlo's eyes widened in surprise—it was Forneus! *"No! Wait!"*

Forneus slashed Arlo's chest with his claws, and this time Arlo spoke his first clear words: "Please, stop! I didn't know!"

"That's the problem with people like you; you know nothing!"

The bear leaned down and bit into Arlo's leg with his powerful jaws, lifting Arlo off the ground and slinging him into the creek. Arlo landed with a splash and raised himself to run, but Forneus was on him again.

He pressed Arlo's chest with both paws, making him dip underneath the water.

"Do you want to know why you are here?" Forneus asked in Arlo's mind.

"Yes! Tell me!" replied Arlo.

The bear opened his mouth and clamped down on Arlo's face. He lifted Arlo by his head, dangling him like a toy before tossing him onto the grass. Arlo landed facedown and moaned in agony.

"I chose you!" bellowed Forneus.

Arlo's world was on fire again, but the intensity hadn't reached its peak. Individual items started combusting around him; fire appeared on the water and disappeared like someone was trying to ignite it. A few surrounding trees started smoking, shooting soot into the night air. Arlo looked at his forearm and saw his skin sizzling like butter in a frying pan.

"Please, Forneus! The fires are coming! I need to feed!"

But Forneus showed no mercy. The bear pressed his face into Arlo's back, gouging his skin with its sharp incisors.

"I wish I could rid myself of your infernal racket, but alas, I cannot. My dreams speak of the approaching storm, and you have an important role to play."

Suddenly the bear reached inside a nearby bush and pulled out a tiny fawn. The small deer cried as it tried to escape, but Forneus was too strong; he quickly broke the fawn's neck, opened his mouth, and stuffed the dead animal inside. Forneus repeatedly chewed until the deer was nothing but mush in his mouth.

With Forneus distracted by eating, Arlo saw his opportunity to run. He jumped up and tried to run into the forest. As soon as he took his first step toward the forest, the bear grabbed Arlo, slammed him to the ground, and sat on his chest. Arlo's eyes bulged in agony as the weight of the great beast smashed his organs, causing black sludge to fill his mouth.

"Where do you think you're going, coward?" asked Forneus.

With deer blood and guts leaking from his full mouth, he threw back his head and laughed. Forneus lifted his broad paw and delivered a thunderous slap across Arlo's face, opening his mouth.

"This should ease your whining," said Forneus.

Forneus moved his bear face close to Arlo's and let the bloody deer mush fall from his mouth. The disgusting mixture landed with a splat on Arlo's face, and Arlo began hungrily sucking it into his mouth.

Forneus climbed off Arlo's chest and sat on the ground to watch him. Like a rabid dog, Arlo ate everything as fast as he could, chewing and swallowing bits and pieces of animal flesh, brains, and bones until it was all gone. Gradually, the fires in the forest were all extinguished, and Arlo felt the burning sensation subside. He sat on the ground watching the bear, its fiery eyes lighting up the grass around them.

"Why am I here?" asked Arlo.

Forneus snorted in frustration, and liquid fire sprayed out of his nostrils, igniting the ground in front of him, causing the fur on his face to burn. He quickly slapped his face until the fire was gone.

"Your lack of patience is annoying," he grumbled, stamping on the ground before him to put out the small fire.

Arlo sat patiently in silence, waiting for Forneus to speak. *"As you've learned, the dead do not sleep, but we are all capable of visions. Some see flashes of their previous lives, but the majority of the undead see the nightmares of their living loved ones."*

"And these visions will happen to me?"

"Certainly, if your family is alive."

"What did you see?"

"In the beginning, I saw my son's nightmares—images of Hell so unsettling, they almost drove me insane. But after the Angel visited, I stopped seeing images of my son's dreams. I think the Angel took pity on me and erased that burden."

"What do you see now?"

"Now I have visions of the future. It is within these dreams that I saw you and Isadora."

The bear rose from the ground and lumbered over to the stream. He looked around for a few moments and then dunked his head into the water, extracting a giant fish. With the fish flopping inside its mouth, Forneus returned to Arlo and plopped down in front of him. He threw back his head and pushed the fish into his mouth—after taking two bites, it was gone.

"The Red Soldiers are coming, and they will kill relentlessly until all human life is gone."

"Red Soldiers? From Hell?"

"They belong to Balam the Demon, third in line for the throne of Hell."

"Balam?"

"It was Balam who tortured me and killed my wife. But he is also the Demon behind the deaths of two teenagers—you and Isadora."

"I don't understand. My best friend, Manuel, murdered me."

"Yes, that's what they wanted you to believe. But Balam used your friend to get to you."

"How is that possible? I don't recall Manuel using Balam's name."

"The creatures of Hell are cunning, but a Demon is the most wicked. Balam didn't approach your friend directly; he used a Mud Creature as an intermediary to hide his identity."

"A Mud Creature?"

"The Mud Creatures worship Demons like teenagers. Killing, stealing, lying—they'll do anything for a seat next to their masters in Hell. Mud Creatures haven't earned their places in Hell's domain, so they live as outcasts of evil, hiding in nightmares, terrorizing people and pushing them to do bad things, hoping a Demon notices them and takes them in.

Arlo's eyes lit up. *"John! John Mudd! He's a Mud Creature!"*

"He is. John caught the attention of Balam, and now Balam is using him as his own. The Demons of Hell have been stealing souls from Heaven using this technique for centuries."

"And you learned all this through a vision?"

"Don't be ridiculous. I've had thousands of visions and learned from each of them."

Arlo was silent for a moment before speaking. *"What does all this have to do with me?"*

"In my vision, I see a young boy and girl standing atop a mountain of dead soldiers. I never see who they are because they are facing away, looking at two enormous headstones. The names on the stones are yours and Isadora's."

Arlo frowned. *"Two headstones? That could mean anything! You brought us back to life because of a fucking dream?"*

"All the visions have come to pass."

Arlo stood and started walking away.

"Your belief is not required," boomed Forneus. *"Time reveals all."*

Arlo stopped and turned to face the bear.

"Why don't you tell me the truth?"

The fire in the bear's eyes grew brighter, and he raised himself on his hind legs. *"Are you calling me a liar?"*

But Arlo didn't flinch. *"I'm dead, Forneus, and so is my fear. I'm not afraid of you."*

The bear opened his mouth and roared at Arlo, but the boy didn't move.

"Maybe an attack from Hell is coming, but that isn't the only reason you raised me from the dead. You owe Heaven a lot of years, don't you?"

The bear sprinted to a nearby tree and angrily swiped at it with his sharp claws, cutting it in half.

"You brought me here because I'm your one chance at erasing those years. How many souls would be spared by defeating Hell's Army? Thousands?"

The fire in the bear's eyes dimmed. Forneus flopped on the ground and sighed. *"Millions,"* Forneus admitted.

"You want me to help you get to your wife in Heaven," said Arlo.

Arlo stood staring at the bear—it looked weak and defeated, like no energy was left.

"It's true. There isn't a day I don't mourn my wife and son. Sometimes when I'm walking in the forest, I catch her scent on a breeze, and I'm depressed for months. You don't know what it's like."

Arlo walked over to the bear and sat down. *"Look, I understand your pain. But peace in death was mine, and you had no right to bring me into this kind of life."*

The bear inhaled, and a deep moan escaped his throat. Arlo turned away to stare at the creek—listening in silence as the mighty beast became a shrunken ball of fragility, sobbing in pain.

After listening to the great beast's cries in silence, Arlo rose to his feet and started walking back to the building. Just as he entered the forest, he heard Forneus's voice in his head.

"My reasons may be selfish, but there is something else you need to consider. The Red Army will be here soon, and because of my deeds, you now have a chance to save the people you love from Hell's wrath. That is a gift that you cannot afford to squander on resentment. Hell is coming, and whomever you love will soon be in their sights."

The words hit their intended target and caused Arlo to pause. After thinking about Forneus's words, Arlo turned toward the city. As he began the long trek through the woods to visit his mother, Arlo didn't notice Isadora kneeling on the ground. She was feasting on the brains of a deer and saw him stumble past. After taking a final bite of deer brains, Isadora followed Arlo through the woods.

12

Bob, The Security Guard Who Got Away

Bob peered nervously out of the blinds at the dark street. After watching the row of cars for several moments, he turned his attention to his neighbors' yards. Bob scrutinized each yard, searching for anything that looked out of the ordinary. He saw that his neighbor, Daniel, had left his sprinkler running and was flooding his yard. The Powells, an elderly couple usually preoccupied with what other neighbors did, had spilled their garbage can in their driveway and hadn't cleaned it up. But beyond those two discrepancies, the other houses appeared normal.

Something moved out of the corner of Bob's eye, and he quickly released the blinds and melted away into the room's darkness. He slowly grabbed his handgun from the table and held it by his side, waiting for someone—or some*thing*—to breach the window. Barely allowing a breath to escape, he remained in the dark, shaking, waiting, preparing for the worst. But nothing came.

Finally, after five minutes of silence, his curiosity got the best of him, and he opened the shades to look out again. Just as he did, a Siberian Husky ran across the lawn, carrying a rubber ball in its mouth. The animal froze for a moment and cast a knowing glance in Bob's direction before trotting around the house and disappearing into the night.

Feeling relieved, Bob let go of the blinds and sat down in his recliner. He grabbed a fresh pack of cigarettes from the open box, twisted off the plastic, and popped a smoke into his mouth.

"I'm probably imagining things," Bob whispered. But inside, he knew he had every right to be afraid. What Bob experienced at his job a week ago was his worst nightmare realized. Bob tried to think of other things, but his mind always returned to the helicopter tarmac and the strange creatures he saw emerge from that helicopter. Bob couldn't reconcile those wicked things with reality—he'd tried continuously, failing every time he looked for a reasonable explanation. But the monsters weren't the most frightening aspect of that night.

"The children," Bob whispered, taking a drag on his cigarette.

He'd never shot anyone before, let alone a child. But they'd attacked him like wild animals, screaming, barking, and growling. Bob had no choice but to shoot them to escape. By the time he made it to the hospital exit, Bob had lost count of how many he had killed. But still, Bob kept firing, emptying his weapon at anything that came at him. He'd recognized some of the boys; some he'd seen in the grocery store, while others were patients he'd interacted with on his shift. But they were all different, their insides hollowed out, replaced with something from Hell.

Bob took his final drag on the cigarette and realized it was gone. He stuffed the butt into the overflowing ashtray and reached for another.

"We're all fucking dead," Bob whispered as he lit another cigarette. Just as he was about to look out the blinds again, the door opened, and his wife walked in. Bob dropped the cigarette, grabbed the gun from the table, and pointed it at her.

"I was thinking about taking Jennifer to the . . ."

Debra saw her husband pointing the weapon at her and dropped the tray on the floor. "Bob, no!" she screamed.

Bob lowered the weapon and shook his head. "Jesus, Deb! I told you to knock! I could've shot you!"

Her heart racing, Debra turned on the light and cleaned up the mess.

"Turn off the fucking light! They might see us!" yelled Bob.

Debra ignored Bob and continued picking up the food.

"Goddamn it, Bob. I've had it! We're going to my mother's house when Jennifer comes home."

Bob stormed over and turned off the light. "You're not taking Jennifer anywhere!"

Debra started crying. "Look at you, Bob! You haven't been to work in days, and you're not eating or sleeping. Now you're stopping us from leaving—it isn't healthy!"

"I knew you didn't believe me!"

"I do! I mean . . . I want to believe you, but how can I when you're acting so crazy?"

"I know what I saw!"

"Then why hasn't your job called? Why hasn't there been any hint of it on the news? Jennifer went to school multiple days and returned home without a scratch. She spent the night at her friend's house and is on her way home now. Meanwhile, you're locked away in this room, acting like a complete psycho. Maybe we need to get you some help."

"Jesus Christ, not that shit again."

"I'm telling you, Bob, something's wrong."

Bob cocked his weapon and looked outside. "Something's wrong? You're goddamned right there is."

Debra left the room and slammed the door behind her while Bob stared out the window, talking to himself. "We can't hole up here much longer. We've got to get out of here soon."

Suddenly the doorbell sounded, and Bob heard voices.

"Fuck!" said Bob. "She didn't pay attention to a fucking thing I've said!"

Holding the handgun, Bob opened the bedroom door, peeked out, and then ran down the stairs. When he reached the bottom, he saw his daughter standing at the bottom, holding an overnight bag.

"Hi, Dad!" said Jennifer.

Bob quickly tucked the handgun into the back of his waist. "Hey, Kiddo! Did you spend the night somewhere?"

"Mom didn't tell you? I stayed at Julie's. It was her birthday, and we had so much studying to do. Coming home didn't make sense, so Mom packed a bag for me and brought it to the school."

"Did she?" Bob frowned disapprovingly at Debra.

"Don't be mad at Mom, Dad. She just wanted to get back to our routine. How are you feeling? Better?"

"A little."

"Good. Well, I'm off to bed. I have a big day tomorrow. Goodnight."

Jennifer kissed both her parents, grabbed her bag, and started walking upstairs to her room. Before she reached the top of the stairs, both parents shot worried looks at one another before turning away—they both felt sick and could barely contain the urge to vomit. Debra took off running to the bathroom while Bob sprinted to the kitchen sink. After emptying the contents of his stomach, he stared at himself through the window's reflection; his face was shiny with sweat, and his eyes were bloodshot.

"Nice way to use the kid to get to us, you fucker!" he cursed.

Bob took the gun out of his pants and placed the muzzle against his temple.

"There's no way you're turning me into one of those things," he whispered.

After thinking for a moment, Bob lowered the weapon, tucked it back into the back of his pants, and splashed water on his face. It occurred to Bob that killing himself wasn't the best decision. Who would protect his family from the monsters if he were gone? Bob vomited again, but this time there was blood in the sink. After wiping his mouth, he stood listening—he could hear Debra throwing up in the other room. Bob walked to the bottom of the stairs and listened to see if his daughter was sick. But after listening for several minutes, he only heard Jennifer gossiping on her cell phone.

Soon Debra emerged from the bathroom. Her skin was gray, and her eyes looked sunken in her head. She walked past Bob and started climbing the stairs. “I don’t feel well. I’m going to bed.”

Bob retched, and Debra turned to look down at him.

“You’d better come to bed too, Bob. It must be some bug going around.”

Bob nodded his head in agreement. “I’ll be up in a minute, babe. Just let me clean up this mess.”

As soon as Debra disappeared, Bob took his gun out and cocked it. He knew he had to kill his wife and daughter before taking his own life.

13

Bob's Fate

Jennifer sat up suddenly and turned on the lamp next to her bed. Her bed was vibrating, and she didn't know why.

"Is it an earthquake?" she asked, watching the water in her fish tank move slightly.

Jennifer climbed out of bed and ran to the window—none of the car alarms were going off, and the other houses were dark. Feeling relieved, she climbed back into bed. After a few moments, she looked at her fish tank again and saw that the water was still.

"It's probably just my imagination."

Jennifer pulled the blanket up to her chin and closed her eyes.

Suddenly something heavy crashed against her bedroom wall, making the water splash out of her fish tank onto the floor.

"Mom!" she yelled.

A more forceful thump sounded, cracking the wall down the middle and making the bookcase fall to the floor.

Jennifer jumped out of bed and ran into the hallway.

"Mom! Dad!" she screamed.

But her parents didn't respond. Jennifer ran to the end of the hallway and grabbed her parents' bedroom door handle.

"AHHHHHH!" Jennifer screamed.

The doorknob was so hot, it burned her hand. Jennifer used her t-shirt and grabbed the handle again. After struggling, the door finally opened.

The room was so hot, Jennifer had to step back; the windows were foggy, and the wallpaper was bubbling. Although the lights were off, a strange red glow lit the room.

"Oh my God," whispered Jennifer.

The room was a mess. Jennifer's parents' bed lay destroyed, a pile of unrecognizable kindling and fabric scattered about the room. Her eyes moved across the floor and fell on two items—her mother's bloody, shredded bra and her father's partially melted gun, lying next to the wall. Jennifer noticed a dripping sound and looked at the wall adjacent to her room; half out of the wall was a human torso, dripping blood on her parents' dresser, while another torso lay nearby with intestines spilling out.

"I . . . I don't understand," cried Jennifer.

Suddenly something moved behind the door, and Jennifer jumped back.

"Mommy? Daddy?" asked Jennifer, backing away from the room. She hoped her parents were behind the door, but she knew it was something much worse. Slowly, two pairs of long stringy red fingers grabbed the side of the door and began pulling it open. Next, four large eyes looked out from behind it.

"AAAHHHHH!" Jennifer screamed before falling to the floor.

Two terrifying creatures stepped out from their hiding place, laughing and cupping their long, spiderlike fingers over their mouths. They were hideously deformed caricatures of human beings with enormous plate-sized watery eyes, muscular bodies, and shiny red skin. Though possessing a human nose and mouth, their faces had blood pouring out of them. Branded on their chests was an eye that blinked and looked around the room. Each monster had four arms—two like humans and two smaller arms sticking out of their shoulders, all filled with dozens of tiny living scorpions that moved beneath their skin. Instead of walking, they slid along the hardwood floors on webbed feet, laughing in a high-pitched giggle that both terrified and taunted.

Jennifer pushed herself along the hardwood floor until her back was against the railing.

"What are you?" she asked. "Where's my mother and father?"

The monsters looked at the girl simultaneously and turned to one another, whispering in a strange language. Finally, they faced her again and screamed, their chests splitting down the center, opening to reveal the dead faces of Bob and Debra tucked inside.

Jennifer saw her parents' faces and passed out. The creatures' bodies closed, and they stepped over the girl with their hoofed feet. With their massive legs, they squatted, crashed through the ceiling, and disappeared into the night.

14

The House

John stood in the dark, taking in the ambiance of the empty house. The place that used to be his home had so much joy and laughter, but now it was just a cold wooden structure, filled with dust and the faint smell of pine oil. Still, John couldn't help but smile as he remembered growing up in the house. His life as Manuel had been the storybook life most kids would kill to have—filled with the pranks of an annoying sister, candy, and friends.

"Friends," John whispered, spotting a familiar corner of the room. He remembered the old brown sofa that was once there, a couch on which he and his best friend, Arlo, used to spend hours playing video games.

"I'm sorry, bro," whispered John. "We should be conquering this world together."

Although he knew Arlo was dead, John couldn't help feeling the regret of taking his friend's life. He missed Arlo, and no matter how many souls he took into his body, nothing could erase the guilt of betraying his best friend.

"Are you okay, my Lord?" asked a voice from behind.

John turned to see the Witch Asura standing in the doorway. "I'm fine. I'm just reminiscing a bit."

"You are thinking of your life as the boy Manuel."

"Yes."

"You cannot waste time thinking of Arlo. His betrayal was a necessary step in fulfilling Lord Balam's wish."

John sighed and walked past the old woman onto the front porch. After taking a deep breath, he opened the gate and stepped onto the street.

"I wonder if they still live here," said John, shoving his hands in his pockets.

Asura exited the gate behind Arlo, looking around nervously as they moved down the dark street. The two walked past several houses until Arlo's house came into view.

Just as they moved within a few feet of the house, the front door opened, and Arlo's father walked out, carrying a garbage bag. As soon as Jamie spotted John, he dropped the garbage on the ground.

"I don't believe it! Manuel, is that you?"

John smiled and moved closer. "It pleases me that you remember, but I'm different now. My name is John."

Jamie looked puzzled. "John? What are you talking about? Did you get a name change or something?"

John chuckled and nodded toward the house. "Is Mrs. Ortega inside? Where's Arlo?"

Jamie's face hardened, and he grabbed the trash bag from the ground. As he was about to respond, terrifying giggles rang out from the shadows.

"What was that?" asked Jamie.

John turned to Asura. "The Huturo are here," he said calmly.

"Yes, my Lord. I sense two of them," replied Asura.

Jamie looked around, confused. "Huturo? What the heck is that? Who is this, your grandmother?"

Asura pulled John close and calmly lifted her palm. A flash of light shot from her hand and wrapped around her and John like a snake before finally exploding into an electrified purple bubble that enveloped them.

"Holy fucking shit!" yelled Jamie, backing away.

Frightened by Asura's bubble, Jamie turned to run back to the house, but stopped—two giant shadows stood lurking, blocking his entrance.

"Manuel, I don't understand. What the hell is going on?" he asked, terrified.

John and Asura remained silent as they watched from inside the bubble. A twisted smile soon appeared on John's face as he remembered all the moments he'd interacted with Arlo's father. John never liked Jamie and remembered Jamie behaving like an arrogant jackass whenever John visited. Jamie was domineering, always intent on showing everyone he was the man of the house, and frequently humiliated his family to prove it. To John, there wasn't a more fitting target to test the killing power of Balam's Huturo soldiers.

As Jamie backed away, the creatures moved out of the moonlight to reveal themselves—two deformed monsters with large plate-sized eyes and red skin stared at him through the darkness. Jamie saw the monsters and started peeing in his pants.

"W-w-what the hell are they?" he asked.

The creatures lifted their heads and sniffed the air; they could smell the fear in Jamie's urine, making them giggle like children. With one set of hands, they tried covering their smiles to hide their glee while the other arms reached out to Jamie like thin tree branches, beckoning him to come closer. They stomped across the grass like cattle, pulling up clumps of soil with their hoofed feet.

As the creatures moved across the yard, Jamie saw the lights in his house turn on. Terrified, he watched as his wife passed by the window into the other room.

"Claire," Jamie whispered, quickly looking away.

Hoping the creatures didn't see the light turn on, Jamie tried to distract them by running past the purple force field to the neighboring house. One of the Huturo gave chase, leaping over the purple force field, while the other monster stopped in front of it, mesmerized by the color. Jamie started banging on the door.

"Please! Open up!"

All of the lights in the house turned on, and a voice yelled down from an upstairs window. "Who the fuck is out there? I have a gun in here, you son of a bitch!"

Jamie recognized the voice. "Tom, it's me, Jamie! Open up!"

"Jamie, is that you? What the hell? It's late. What do you want?"

As the Huturo grew closer, Jamie began to panic. He spotted a large stone on the ground, picked it up, and smashed the windowpane closest to the door.

"Son of a bitch!" cursed his neighbor.

Jamie could hear his neighbor fumbling around, searching for his rife. When Jamie's neighbor started running down the stairs, it was too late—the Huturo had reached Jamie. With one of its claws, the creature latched onto Jamie's throat and began squeezing until blood poured from his nose and eyes. Its three other hands firmly held Jamie's torso in place. Then, with one powerful motion, the Huturo lifted, tearing Jamie's head off his body with the spine still attached, dangling and dripping with blood.

Suddenly the house's front door opened, and Jamie's neighbor appeared, dressed in a stained t-shirt and boxers, holding his shotgun.

"You crazy son of a bitch! How dare you come to . . ."

The middle-aged man looked at the Huturo holding Jamie's head and tried slamming the door shut. But the Huturo splintered the door and walked into the house without effort. The man fell to his knees, trembling while the monster towered above him, eyes wide and covered in blood, giggling uncontrollably. It dropped Jamie's head in front of the man and covered its mouth to hide its laugh.

"I'm going to Hell, aren't I?" the sobbing old man asked.

Suddenly the creature opened its arms to reveal its chest, and the flesh slowly began tearing down the middle until it opened, showing the two faces of Bob and Debra, the husband and wife they'd killed earlier. Suddenly the two dead faces opened their eyes and shrieked. With their spinal cords still attached to the Huturo, the heads shot out of the Huturo's chest and began biting the man's face. The man screamed horribly as the possessed faces tore the skin from his face and neck, continuing to eat until he fell silent.

15

Fortification

John stared at the Huturo standing in front of the force field. The creature seemed more brutal than the creatures he conjured from Hell —twisted with a sense of killing that the others lacked. The beast stared at John and Asura with its enormous eyes, becoming distracted as electricity moved through the purple bubble. Finally, it reached out to grab John and was instantly shocked by the force field. The Huturo recoiled in surprise, and attempted it again with a different hand. This time the electrical current of the bubble was more violent, burning the creature's hand and sending the smell of burning flesh into the night air. The Huturo's eyes filled with tears, and it screamed angrily at John before throwing its entire body at the force field. A massive bolt of electricity struck the creature in its chest, sending it sliding out onto the street and crashing against a car. The Huturo fell to its knees, gasping for air. Eventually, it sat on the ground, defeated and visibly out of breath.

"It's tired," said John.

One of the monster's smaller arms fell from its shoulder and began squirming on the pavement, transforming into a scorpion, then a spider, before bursting into flame and melting away. The Huturo started furiously sucking for air and fell on its back. Its large eyes turned black and then exploded, sending baby spiders scattering onto the street. Suddenly the creature's body burst into flame and disappeared.

Asura waved her hand and deactivated the force field as John walked over to the stained pavement and stared at the remains of the Huturo.

"Weak," said John.

Asura nodded her head in agreement. "What will we do, my Lord?"

"We need to find a way to make the transformations of the Huturo permanent."

Suddenly there was a sound behind them, and they turned to see the other Huturo walk out of the house down the street. With its chest open and the heads of the husband and wife flailing, the creature fell to the ground. It saw John and Asura watching and tried to stand, but it wasn't strong enough and fell back to the pavement. The heads detached from the Huturo's chest and slithered down the street toward John, but they didn't get far—large pustules appeared on their faces and exploded, sending hundreds of spiders scurrying into their eyes and mouths. In seconds they were nothing but skulls lying in the street. The Huturo, chest open and unable to move, growled at John and Asura before disintegrating into a thick black fluid.

John turned to Asura. "Call the Witches now."

Asura reached into her robe and pulled out a glass jar containing a wrinkled human hand submerged in thick green fluid. She opened the container, lifted the hand, and inspected it closely.

"With the Black Magic of Dorosha, I summon you," she whispered.

Asura grabbed the pinky finger, broke it off, and put it in her mouth. She slowly began chewing, and her eyes turned emerald green. She started chewing faster, and her face twisted in disgust. Finally, she swallowed, and her eyes returned to normal.

"It is done, my Lord. By the setting of the sun, the Witches of Blood Mountain will stand before you."

"Are you sure?"

"If they do not arrive, the young Witch will descend to The Caves of Trango, where she will spend an eternity in darkness with the Stone Worms feasting on her flesh."

"Excellent."

Just as John turned to leave, he heard a door open. It was Claire. "Oh my God. Manuel? Is that you?" she asked.

Asura turned to John. "I sense other Huturo in the area."

Asura extended her arm again, and the force field returned. Claire stared at the pair, terrified. She immediately retreated inside the house and slammed the door.

"We have one more stop before returning to the hospital," John said with a wicked smile.

With the Witch following closely behind, John walked across the yard to the door and went inside.

16

Parental Rights

The streets were mysteriously empty when Arlo looked out from the edge of the forest. He decided not to take the same route to the back of his parents' house because he feared his father would be armed and waiting. Arlo staggered across the street and ran to a yard several spots away from his mother's house. As he was about to run to the neighboring home, Isadora emerged from the bushes.

"Arlo! It's me, Isadora!" she said inside his head.

Arlo stumbled over to her hiding spot.

"What are you doing here?"

"I saw you running through the forest, and I followed you. What's going on?"

"That jerk, Forneus. He told me something bad's about to happen."

"The Red Army? Yeah, he told me about that, too."

Arlo hadn't thought of it earlier, but Isadora never talked about her family.

"Did you warn your family?" asked Arlo.

Isadora looked away. *"What family? All I had was my mom and dad, and you know what happened to them."*

"You mean you don't have any family? No cousins or aunts? Uncles?"

"Sure I do, but I've never met them. Mom told me she had a brother, but he's a truck driver, always on the road. I heard I have cousins in

Florida, but no one communicated with us. Something about my father being abused and cutting people off. Who knows? Everyone has the right to be alone, I guess."

"That's messed up."

"Yeah, families are fucked up like that."

Arlo ran into another yard and waited until Isadora caught up.

"What's the plan?"

"What do you mean?"

"Didn't your dad try to blow your head off the last time? How are you going to convince them to hide?"

Arlo shrugged and stared at the house next to his mother's; the door was open, and something was lying on the doorstep.

"Well?" asked Isadora.

Arlo turned and looked at her. *"What?"*

"How are you going to convince them to move? Look at you. Your guts are hanging out from the gunshot wounds. How are you going to communicate? They can't speak with their thoughts like us, and the rot in your throat is getting worse. Soon all you'll be able to do is moan."

Arlo ignored Isadora and crept closer to his neighbor's house. The object on the doorstep looked familiar—like a human head. Isadora moved next to him and continued her conversation.

"Even if you could speak with your parents, what would you say? 'Hi, Mom, I'm a zombie, and there's about to be an invasion from Hell. Run and hide.'"

"Jesus, Isadora! Shut up!" snapped Arlo. *"Something's wrong. What's that over there?"*

Arlo ran through the darkness to the yard and slowly began inching toward the door. As he got closer, he saw blood splattered on the ground and the house.

"Wow! What do you suppose happened?" asked Isadora.

But Arlo didn't respond. He spotted a head attached to a spinal cord lying next to a lawn chair. Soon Arlo saw the victim's corpse. The clothing looked familiar, but he didn't know why. Finally, with his foot, Arlo kicked the head, and it turned over—it was his father.

"Daaaaadddy!" Arlo cried.

His knees buckled, and he fell to the ground sobbing while Isadora stood over him, her eyes filling with tears.

"This is your father?" she asked inside his head.

But Arlo's only response was another moan. "Noooooo," he cried.

Arlo grabbed his father's head and held it in his lap, caressing it, rocking back and forth.

"Don't go, Daddy. Please! I need you!"

As Jamie's eyes stared up into nothingness, Arlo's tears began falling, dripping on the dead man's face. Isadora watched as Arlo became inconsolable, crying and speaking to his father as if he were alive.

"Remember that time we went fishing, and I caught that turtle? I'll never forget that day. We spent all day on that boat, and that's all we caught."

Isadora was touched. She'd never seen Arlo so emotional, like a child lost in the wilderness. Although he was holding his dead father, Isadora felt a powerful urge to embrace Arlo and ease his suffering. Although the moment was macabre and depressing, she felt something powerful inside—Isadora was in love with Arlo.

Suddenly Isadora heard giggling in the forest behind them. *"Um, Arlo? We'd better get out of here. Is your mom inside?"*

Arlo's eyes widened in surprise. *"Mom!"*

Arlo laid his father's head on the porch and sprinted across the street to his house. Without hesitation, he burst through the door.

"Moooom," Arlo moaned.

There was no response.

Arlo ran upstairs and searched the bedrooms—his mother wasn't there. He stumbled downstairs, ran into the kitchen, and froze. There on the linoleum floor was a large blood stain. Arlo fell to his knees and started sobbing again.

"She's dead," he cried.

Isadora peered over Arlo and saw the large puddle of blood. *"You don't know she's dead. Where's the body?"*

Arlo looked up at Isadora, tears streaming down his face. *"Are you fucking kidding me? Do you see all of this blood? She's dead! Everyone is fucking dead!"*

Suddenly the floor began vibrating, and Isadora grabbed the wall. *"Let's get out of here, Arlo! Something's coming!"*

But Arlo continued staring at the bloodstained floor without moving. *"Damn it all. My family's dead, so I may as well join them."*

Suddenly Isadora heard laughter coming from behind the house. She ran to the backdoor and looked out—dozens of shadows were moving around in the backyard. With one swift motion, Isadora grabbed Arlo by his shirt and threw him through the house. Arlo landed in the living room and slid into a coffee table, knocking it over.

"We're leaving! Now!"

Arlo looked up at Isadora, tears streaming down his face, and slowly raised himself from the floor. Isadora grabbed his arm and pulled him out the front door. Just as they exited, the back of the house exploded, and dozens of Huturo poured in. One of the creatures lifted its head and sniffed the air, picking up the scent of the teenagers. It ran past the others and onto the lawn, but the teens were gone.

17

Indentured Servitude, Maybe

"Bitch!"

A mob of children surrounded the three hooded women standing on the hospital lawn while Asura stood on the stairs, watching them.

"Let them approach," Asura said.

The crowd opened, and the women headed to the front. They stopped at the bottom of the stairs and lowered their hoods to reveal themselves—three women who looked more like teenagers than elderly women, hundreds of years old.

Asura chuckled. "I see you're using Black Magic to maintain your youthful appearance. Good. Anything to get a husband, I suppose," she snapped sarcastically.

The youngest woman raised her hand wrapped in black silk.

"Look at what you've done to me. You're nothing but a thirsty-ass bitch, mad because your old leathery face couldn't attract a partner if your life depended on it."

One of the women touched the young woman on the arm, attempting to calm her. After a few moments, she spoke to Asura.

"Excuse us, Lady Asura. I'm Indigo, as I'm sure you remember. Penny has developed an affinity for the dialogue of the current generation, and her words may sometimes seem insulting. Please, excuse us."

"*Seem?*" asked Penny. "There's no *seem* about it. Fuck that bitch!"

Asura removed the jar from her robe and held it high. Inside the green liquid was the woman's wrinkled hand—minus one finger.

"Oh, what some people wouldn't give to pluck the strings of a violin."

Penny became furious and tried to attack Asura, but the other two women held her back.

"Let's see how tough you are without cheating. You had to wait until I was sleeping to sneak in and cut off my hand. You're not a sorceress; you're just a lowlife, bottom-barrel, old-school Witch. Give me my hand and fight me straight up—my magic against yours. I'll split your skull with dragon fire and bury that thing you call a face at the bottom of the Mariana Trench!"

Asura sighed and shook the jar. "Alas, some people have no appreciation for the violin. But I heard you lose the ability to wipe your ass after losing three fingers—isn't that worse?"

Penny launched herself at Asura again, but her sisters once more held her back.

"We don't have time for immature fighting," said Indigo. "What is it that you request of us, Lady Asura?"

Suddenly John stepped out of the hospital doors and walked to Asura's side. "Asura summoned you at my request. My name is John."

"We know who you are," replied Penny.

"Tell us what you want," demanded Indigo.

John walked down the stairs and stood before the three women. "Rain."

Indigo stared at John in disbelief while her other sister spoke.

"Hi, John. I'm Inez. Lady Asura tortured my sister and brought us here for what? Rain?"

Inez's words ignited Penny's anger, and she glared at Asura.

"You see? I told you that old bag is out of her mind. Fuck the hand. Just kill that bitch!"

John raised his hand and spoke softly. "There will be none of that. What I request is not ordinary water; I ask for rain to cover all the land for thirty days—to make my master's soldiers permanent."

"Who is your master?" asked Inez.

The three women looked at one another nervously. Finally, Penny spoke. "Are you referring to . . . ."

Inez immediately pulled Penny close and interrupted. "Don't! Any sorceress who speaks his name risks banishment to the Red Planet," she warned.

Penny turned back to John. "He knows who we mean. It's him, isn't it?"

John smiled. "Yes."

The three women stepped away from John and whispered amongst themselves. After a few moments, they faced John again.

"We require the flesh of one of the Demon's soldiers," said Inez.

"Are they here?" Indigo nervously asked.

John turned and walked away from the women to the stairs. "They are not here, but they'll be along shortly."

Penny stepped forward. "We will do it under one condition. I need my hand returned to me."

John turned to Asura and smiled. "What do you think, Asura? Shall we return Penny's hand?"

Asura smiled. "Certainly. But only after the rain begins."

John and Asura turned and walked back into the building.

The three women sat down on the lawn.

"You watch," whispered Penny. "That old hag is going to trick us."

"For sure," replied Inez.

"Let's do what she says and wait until she makes her move," whispered Indigo. "She's too preoccupied with that boy and hasn't read the stones yet."

The three sisters looked at one another and spoke in unison: "By the time she discovers the truth about Forneus, it'll be too late."

18

A Son's Reprieve

Isadora was worried. It had been six hours since they returned, and Arlo still hadn't eaten. She knew he was feeling the effects of the Sun Oil, and his skin was starting to burn. If he continued drowning in sadness, he'd burn and melt away.

Still, Arlo hadn't moved. Occasionally, a garbled sigh escaped his throat, and Isadora longed to hold him—she knew Arlo was hiding his tears in the dark room and wanted to cheer him up, to stop him from hurting. Isadora understood the loneliness Arlo felt more than anyone in the world; that dreadful feeling of emptiness, the realization of being alone in a strange world with no one to call your family. Isadora had felt the same thing a few days after she led her parents to their demise. She recalled feeling both ashamed and lonely. Fortunately, Forneus was there to redirect her fate. And so she wanted to do the same thing for Arlo.

Isadora lifted the head of the dead man lying in front of her and hit it with a stone; the body was still warm, and her victim's frail bones broke without effort. She stuck her hand into the top of his head and scooped out a handful of brains. She was about to eat them when she turned to Arlo.

"Hey, Arlo. Do you want some?"

Arlo looked at her briefly, then turned away.

"Don't worry. I didn't kill the guy—he saw me walking in the forest and had a heart attack. I should feel bad for the guy, but I don't. He was out there hunting for sport."

Arlo remained silent.

Isadora put the handful of slimy brain matter into her mouth. *"Come on, Arlo. Try some. This guy's brains are as sweet as cherry pie."*

Isadora licked her fingers clean and grabbed Arlo's hand. *"I'm sorry about your dad."*

Arlo sighed again, and a tear landed on the back of Isadora's hand.

"You've got to be strong, Arlo. I know things are horrible, but you've got to have hope."

Arlo lifted his head and turned to Isadora. *"Hope?"*

"Sure. Your mom could still be alive."

Arlo slammed his fist on the ground. *"There's no hope. She's fucking dead just like the rest of them."*

Arlo pushed Isadora's hand away and lied on the floor.

Just as he did, a dull light appeared at the entrance, and Forneus walked in. He clambered over to Arlo and stood above him. *"What's wrong?"*

Isadora motioned to the corner of the room, and Forneus followed. *"We found his parents. They're dead."*

"Both of them?"

"I think so. We found Arlo's father's body, but when we searched for his mother, we only saw a blood stain."

"How did they die?"

"I think it was the Red Soldiers. No?"

Forneus sat down on the floor, and the snakes in his chest slithered around, making the room brighter.

"The Soldiers of Hell are here, for sure. I spotted them on the north side of the forest. Luckily, I had taken the form of a fox and got away before they spotted me. They've overrun the city completely and will be everywhere in two days."

Isadora looked worried. *"What are we going to do, Forneus?"*

"No matter what happens, you can't let the soldiers capture you. If they do, you won't go to the Great Sleep. They'll let the Sun Oil burn you and take your soul to Hell, where you'll be a slave for all eternity."

"How do we stop them?"

"We build an army of our own."

"An army? But how?"

"Somehow I've got to use my powers to resurrect as many souls as possible without being seen."

"How many souls have you raised in a day?"

"Back when I was motivated by Hell's lie, I raised fifty in one day."

"Fifty?! There's an army out there!"

Forneus rubbed his head, and the worms inside his skull began screeching.

"There are three women I know that could help, but I'm not sure I can convince them."

"Where are they?"

"They live in the nearby forest."

"Are you sure you can make it there without being seen?"

"Maybe. But even if I convince the women to help, it will be useless if we don't fix what's wrong here." Forneus nodded toward Arlo lying on the floor. *"Arlo is the key to fighting Hell's Soldiers. We have no chance at success if we don't fix him."*

"How do we do that?"

"There's something I didn't tell you. When the Angel from Heaven visited me to inform me of Hell's deception, the Angel took pity on me. She didn't say it, but I knew she thought Heaven's penalty was excessive. The Angel told me there had never been another who had to endure such a stiff punishment. She was certain I would go mad or turn to Hell. To ease my suffering, she gave me access to the Priming Fields."

"What are those?"

"The Angel explained it to me like this: After the Great Sleep, souls receive their call for judgment. The accounting of all good deeds and sins happens, and when the soul receives a favorable review and atonement for

their sins is complete, they begin the final trip along the road to Heaven's Gates. The Priming Fields is the last stop on that road—it's a place of rejuvenation that refreshes travelers before they get to Heaven."

"Wow. Who's there now?"

"No one. It's been inactive for hundreds of years."

"Why?"

"The second judgment of man hasn't occurred. When that happens, I'm sure it'll have many souls. But it's not being used now. That is why the Angel granted me six visits—to use it whenever my soul is damaged."

"And you want to send Arlo there?"

"The both of you."

"Me?"

"I see how you look at Arlo. I hear the love in your voice."

Isadora lowered her head bashfully. *"It's nothing."*

"The two of you are bound to one another in life and death; it only makes sense that your love for him grows. But that's not the only reason I'm sending you. I sense damage to your spirit; you've become more violent and animalistic. Traveling to the Priming Fields will reeducate you on the purpose of your existence and the boundaries between good and evil."

"When do we go?"

"Now. Hell's Army is growing by the thousands every hour, and in my visions, I've learned more about Arlo's part in this—he's the leader, and when he falls, so does the world. We have no time to waste."

"Where will you be?"

"I'll try to reach the sisters on the mountain."

Forneus stood and walked across the room to Arlo. *"Arlo, I'm going to help your suffering, okay?"*

Arlo looked up at the towering skeleton. *"Don't you touch my fucking parents, you asshole!"*

Arlo lunged at Forneus and missed, landing on his face. Forneus grabbed the back of his shirt and righted him.

"Don't worry, boy. I have no intention of raising your family from the dead. I'm sending you and Isadora to a special place."

Arlo sighed and turned away.

"Does it look like I'm up for a fucking road trip? My family is dead! Please leave me alone and let the Sun Oil burn me to Hell. I don't give a shit anymore."

Forneus grabbed Arlo by the scruff of his neck and turned to Isadora. *"Insert your hand into Arlo's ribcage."*

The words got Arlo's attention, and his eyes widened. *"Wait, what?"*

Forneus ignored Arlo and nodded to Isadora. *"Go ahead. Proceed."*

Isadora inserted her hand into the opening in Arlo's chest.

"Now, Arlo, you do the same with Isadora."

Arlo looked afraid. *"Why? What are you doing?"*

The snakes in Forneus's chest lit up and began thrashing wildly. *"Do as I say, boy. There isn't much time."*

Slowly, Arlo pushed his hand into Isadora's chest.

"Now, push through the organs until you reach the heart. Once you reach it, hold it firmly and don't let go."

Arlo started trembling. *"Won't that kill us?"*

Isadora shook her head and sighed. *"We're dead, Arlo. Remember? Your heart isn't beating."*

Arlo leaned forward and began pushing through Isadora's organs, grimacing as he searched for her heart. Soon, thick black liquid poured out of her body onto his arm.

"I . . . I can't reach it," Arlo complained.

Forneus placed his hand behind the teenagers' backs and slid them together. *"Find it,"* boomed Forneus.

As the two teens searched, they stared into each other's eyes—Arlo, entirely disgusted by the odor of death on Isadora's breath, and Isadora, filled with emotion, wishing Arlo would kiss her.

Finally, the two grabbed one another's hearts and turned to Forneus.

"Now what?" asked Arlo.

"Now close your eyes," replied Forneus.

Both Arlo and Isadora closed their eyes.

"Listen to me carefully. When you exit the building into the fields, the sun will rise on your left, travel across the sky, and set on your right—use the sun as a clock. Do not wait until the sun sets. Try to reenter the building to leave when the sun starts its descent. If you are within the Priming Fields at nightfall, every evil creature within five miles of this building will try to gain entry and take you to Hell. You are the undead and are visiting the Priming Fields without receiving judgment, breaking the contract Heaven and Hell made on the souls of the undead. You must avoid overstaying your visit to the Priming Fields at all costs. Do you understand?"

"Yes," replied Isadora.

Arlo remained silent.

"I have never given another soul access to the Priming Fields, so bear with me. I will send my powers of resurrection into you, and it will burn."

Forneus stood over the teenagers and extended his arms. His head's worms thrashed wildly, screaming and flashing various colors before hardening like concrete and sinking to the bottom of his skull. Suddenly Forneus's hands filled with electricity and shot two enormous thunderbolts into the top of Isadora's and Arlo's skulls, causing the teens' bodies to stiffen before falling unconscious.

19

Touching the Storm

Penny looked at the unconscious Huturo floating in the air and turned to her sisters in disgust. "You guys have the easy job," she said. "Why do I have to touch it?"

"Because we can't complete the job without your help," replied Inez. "Its hands are tied. Go ahead and cut it!"

Penny moved closer to the monster and saw tiny scorpions moving beneath its skin. "Fuck! It's crawling with scorpions!"

Indigo sighed. She pulled Penny away from the monster, tossed her robe aside, and removed a large knife from her waist.

"Jeez, Penny. Do you have to act like a baby all the time? I'll cut it, but you're going up in the clouds to freeze your ass off, not me."

Indigo sliced a chunk of meat off the creature's back and dropped the knife; the piece of red flesh fell to the ground, covered in scorpions. Suddenly the Huturo opened its eyes and roared angrily at the women.

"He's awake!" yelled Penny. "Shit, Indigo. I thought you said you knocked him out."

"I did, but he's too strong."

The creature grew angrier, hissing and biting at the girls as it tried to break free. Inez extended her palm, and a blue energy whip shot out of her hand and wrapped around the creature's neck.

"Hold him, Inez!" shouted Penny.

"What do you think I'm doing?" replied Inez.

Inez yanked harder on the whip and started taking steps around the creature, hoping to make the whip tighter on its neck. "You're not going anywhere, you bastard!" she yelled.

The monster's eyes widened, and it mimicked Inez's voice. "You're not going anywhere, you bastard!" the creature repeated.

The words surprised Inez, and the grip on the whip loosened. The creature saw its opportunity and jerked its head, sending Inez sailing across the yard. Indigo released a burst of energy from her hand that struck the monster in its chest, electrocuting it and making the beast fall unconscious. Indigo raised her other hand and shot a second line of energy from her fingertips that wrapped around the Huturo's hands.

"Inez, you okay?" yelled Penny.

Inez stood and brushed the dirt off her robe. "I'm fine. Grab the flesh. It's your turn."

Penny walked over to the flesh lying on the ground and held her hand over it.

"Deep thoughts, wet places, and golden fire. *Sharuzomina-te-farva!*"

A transparent sphere appeared on Penny's fingertip and dropped beside the pile of flesh. A few scorpions on the ground tried to attack the bubble, and shocks of electricity immediately vaporized them. The ball landed on the meat and absorbed it before rising from the ground, transforming into a black orb before reaching Penny's hand.

"Okay, Inez. Do it!" yelled Penny.

Inez pointed her open palms at Penny and shot her in the chest with energy.

Penny's body slowly began fading, spinning faster and faster. "Wish me luck, girls," she said. "Shit! It's probably cold as a polar bear's balls up there."

Penny's body didn't melt away but became a white cloud. Suddenly she shot into the air, holding the black orb in the center. When Penny was high enough, she yelled back down to her sisters. "Any day, girls!"

Inez and Indigo aimed their palms at Penny and began chanting. "Stone, darkness, and heavy rain. *Pinturosha-libba-dosh!*"

Suddenly the sisters' bodies began glowing, and their hands burst into flame.

"Okay! Throw it!" yelled Inez to Penny.

Penny tossed the orb into the clouds over the hospital, and her sisters shot blasts of energy into the ball, causing it to explode. As particles rained down from the sky, Penny appeared in her human form and started falling from the sky. On her way down, she cupped her hand over her mouth and blew, creating a gray fog that spread like an enormous blanket. Penny didn't have time to stop her fall and crashed onto the ground with a thud.

"Penny!" yelled Indigo, rushing to her side. "Are you okay?"

Penny rolled over and sat up. "Ow, who dropped that car on my head? I'm never doing that shit again."

Indigo and Inez lifted their sister off the ground and looked up; lightning flashed, and thunder rumbled across the sky. A drop of liquid hit Inez on the head, and she turned to look at the Huturo.

"Guys, we'd better get out of here before the rain starts. Once the water hits the Huturo, we won't be able to control it."

Penny looked up at the sky, and a drop of the liquid landed on her face. She wiped it off and looked at it on her fingertip. "Yuck! It's as thick as snot."

Penny placed her finger under her nose and sniffed. "Ew! It smells like vomit!"

Suddenly the clouds released a rumble, and the clouds exploded in a deluge of rain. The Huturo opened its eyes and quickly removed its restraints.

"We're out of here!" yelled Inez, pulling her sisters away from the monster.

Penny tore away from Inez's grasp and headed for the hospital entrance.

"Penny!" yelled Indigo. "We've got to get out of here!"

"Not without what they promised me!" replied Penny.

When Penny ran up to them, John and Asura were standing at the top of the stairs, watching the rain pour from the sky.

"It is done. Now give me what you promised."

Asura stared at Penny with a smirk on her face. "You did *something*, but how do we know the spell works?"

Penny made a fist, and Asura noticed.

"Oh, look, John. The little girl made a fist with her one good hand. Oh, well, one is better than none, I suppose."

John looked at Asura and nodded. "Give it to her. A deal is a deal."

Reluctantly, Asura reached underneath her robe and retrieved the jar. "Here you go."

Asura held out the jar for Penny to take it. As soon as Penny reached for it, Asura let the jar slip, and it crashed to the ground.

"You fucking bitch!"

"Oh, I'm sorry. I'm a little clumsy sometimes. Here, let me help you."

Asura reached down and picked up the glass-covered hand.

"Let me clean off this glass."

Asura grabbed the fingers, twisted them around until they all broke, and then dropped them on the ground.

John sighed. "Asura, was that necessary?"

Fuming, Penny bit her bottom lip and retrieved her gnarled hand from the ground. When she stood, Penny flexed her nostrils twice. "Excuse me, Lady Asura. I think you have a booger in your nose."

Asura remained motionless, staring at Penny. She tried to stay calm, but eventually, she flinched and wiped at her nose. As soon as she did, Asura's nose ballooned, and she began flailing around, swiping at it. Suddenly the head of a bat popped out from her nose, and next its enormous wings tore a huge gash into Asura's nostril.

John remained stoic, unfazed by the childish behavior. "Take your item and leave before I become angry."

Penny ran down the stairs to her sisters. Indigo clapped her hands together, and the three women were gone in a flash of light.

20

Winding Down

Arlo woke up in darkness on a hard cold floor. After a few moments, he heard someone breathing beside him. Arlo knew it was Isadora and tried speaking to her with his mind. But the words never came. Arlo focused and tried thinking of complete sentences, but he still heard nothing. Frustrated, Arlo opened his mouth and spoke.

"Isadora, is that you?" he asked. Arlo was surprised to hear his voice echoing in the room; there was no cracking or variations in pitch.

"Yeah, I'm here," responded Isadora.

Isadora's voice surprised Arlo even more than his own; her voice was silky like cream poured from a glass. He'd become so accustomed to hearing her voice echoing in his mind that he forgot how she'd sounded when they were at school.

Arlo climbed to his feet and looked around.

"Can you see anything?" asked Isadora.

"No. Everything's dark," responded Arlo.

As Arlo stood, gathering his bearings, he noticed his dizziness was gone, and he no longer had to struggle to maintain his balance. Arlo reached down, felt for Isadora's arm, and pulled her to her feet.

"Wow, Arlo. We sound like normal people."

"Yeah, I know."

After adjusting his eyes, Arlo spotted a light coming from underneath a door on the other side of the room.

"Look, Isadora. Do you see that?"

"It's a door."

Together they stumbled through the darkness to the door, and after feeling around for the handle, Arlo opened it. As soon as he did, a mighty wind sucked them out and sent them flying. They landed on a patch of rocks, water hitting them from all directions.

"Isadora!" Arlo yelled.

But she didn't hear him—another wind gust picked her up and tossed her a few feet away. Arlo ran to Isadora and grabbed her arm. When he pulled her up, another gust of wind filled with salty, stinging water smashed into them and sent them both spinning along the ground.

"Arlo!" screamed Isadora, clinging to his arm.

But Arlo couldn't reply—the wind took his breath away before he could utter a word. Unable to hear one another, Arlo pointed in the direction of the room. He grabbed Isadora's arm, and they started running when suddenly, Isadora pulled away.

"Arlo!" she yelled. "It's not there!"

Arlo stared at the space in disbelief. Water spraying in his face, he turned in a circle to see where they were. They were on a small island in the middle of a raging ocean, water surrounding them.

"NO!" Arlo yelled.

Arlo was furious—Forneus had lied to them. There were no beautiful landscapes or places to ease his pain—only a different version of suffering within a vicious hurricane trying to rip them apart. The teens wrapped their arms around each other and stood in the storm crying, aware of Forneus's betrayal and unsure how to free themselves from the lie.

Suddenly they heard a sound much louder than thunder. Slowly, they turned around.

"Arlo," cried Isadora.

"No," replied Arlo.

Rushing at them from far out in the ocean was a massive tsunami. The wave was so big, it sucked in the storm clouds above it, destroying them as it sped toward the island. Arlo quickly turned around in search of cover but felt even more helpless—multiple tsunamis were racing at them from different directions.

Arlo wrapped his arms around Isadora and squeezed.

"I guess this is it for us!" he yelled.

Suddenly Isadora pushed him away and looked out into the ocean. "I feel so sleepy, Arlo. Do you?"

Isadora's words shocked Arlo and drowsiness fell on him like a ton of bricks. He started swaying and felt his knees weaken as he struggled to keep his eyes open.

"I'm so sleepy," yelled Arlo.

Ignoring the approaching waves, Isadora lied on the rocks and closed her eyes. "Me, too," she whispered.

Arlo tried keeping himself upright, but his knees finally gave out, and he fell to the ground. Just as the tsunamis converged on the island in one towering wave of water, Isadora and Arlo were sound asleep.

21

The Real You

"Stop bothering me, Mom. Give me five more minutes," mumbled Arlo.

Arlo turned over and tried to ignore the interruption but discovered that he couldn't—something wet was splashing his face.

"Really, Mom? You're splashing me with water now?"

Arlo reached for his blanket, but it wasn't there. Feeling frustrated, he sat up.

"Who's the immature one now? I don't bother you when you . . ."

Arlo felt something heavy moving across his chest, and he opened his eyes—a tiny puppy was sitting on his chest, staring at him curiously.

"Hey. Who are you?" asked Arlo.

The puppy tilted its head and continued staring at the boy as if trying to figure him out.

"Where'd you come from?" asked Arlo, reaching out to pet the dog.

The puppy immediately rushed forward and started licking his face.

"HAHAHAHAHA," laughed Arlo hysterically.

"Arf! Arf! Arf!" replied the dog between licks.

Arlo brushed the dog away and stood up to look around. He was alone in an open green field of strange vegetation he didn't recognize. There were sizeable fragrant plants shaped like sunflowers spraying mist in the air that smelled like candy apples, while other plants looked like something out of an artistic nightmare—colorful, twisted, and contorted.

Arlo looked up at the sky and saw the sun creeping slowly across pink, orange, and yellow clouds, leaving a trail of sparkling dust behind as it moved.

"Arf!" barked the dog.

Arlo realized the dog was trying to get his attention.

"What is it?"

Suddenly the dog sprinted across the field toward a patch of dense plants. Just as it was about to enter, the plants moved aside for the dog, and it disappeared inside.

"Hey!" yelled Arlo. "Where are you going?"

Arlo ran across the field and into the patch of vegetation, where he saw the dog sitting on the ground, waiting for him to enter. As soon as the puppy saw Arlo, it ran off again.

"Slow down!" yelled Arlo.

Arlo followed the dog around several large trees, made another turn, and arrived at an enormous waterfall.

"Wow," whispered Arlo.

The waterfall was colossal; a powerful water current poured down from a source beyond the clouds in the sky. There was no thunderous pounding of splashing water landing on the rocks. Instead, the liquid fell into a large basin filled with smooth stones, soundless, before being sent out into the vegetation along thin aqueducts.

"Arf! Arf! Arf!" barked the puppy. It looked at Arlo and then the pool of water as if motioning him to enter.

"You want me to enter?" asked Arlo.

"Arf!" responded the dog.

Cautiously, Arlo moved forward, removed his clothing, and stepped into the water; the water was warm and sent a thrust of pleasure through his body so intense, he fell to his knees. Chest deep in the waterfall, he closed his eyes and crawled forward until the stream of water splashed on his face. After a few seconds, Arlo wiped the water from his face and opened his eyes.

The pool of water around him had transformed into a shimmering pool of gold, lighting up everything around it. Surprised, Arlo stood, wiped his eyes, and looked at the liquid again. Soon he heard people laughing. The giggles tickled him, and Arlo, too, started laughing, unsure of the source of the happiness. He looked down into the golden water and was shocked.

"Mom! Dad!"

Arlo saw his mother's and father's reflection in the water, and a much younger version of himself—it was a moment they'd shared as a family when they had tried baking a cake together and forgotten about it, smoking up the house.

"Who was watching the cake?" he asked, mouthing the exact words he'd asked his mother. As if speaking directly to Arlo from the reflection, Arlo's mother pointed to him with a smile and responded, "You know who!"

The images of the moment slowly faded away and left Arlo standing, waiting for the memory to reappear. But it never did. Still smiling and filled with calm, Arlo exited the pool.

"It surprised me, too," said a voice from the side of the basin.

Arlo looked up and saw Isadora standing before him—or so he thought. Although the person standing before him had all the same mannerisms as the girl he knew, Isadora was drastically different; her entire body was as transparent as glass, and she had no color to her skin. Isadora maintained the same facial features but appeared different; her face constantly moved, distorting, fading in and out, like seeing a reflection when walking past a window. Arlo could tell Isadora was nude, but he couldn't see her body explicitly; a soft violet light glowed in the center of her torso.

Arlo was about to step out of the pool but became nervous when he saw his clothes sitting at the edge of the waterfall.

"You haven't looked at yourself, have you?" asked Isadora, smiling.

Arlo nervously looked down at his hand and sighed in surprise—his body was crystal with a warm blue light shining over his heart.

"Why are we like this?" asked Arlo, surveying his new body.

"I don't know," replied Isadora. "Maybe this is our soul."

"Should I put on my clothing?"

"I didn't put on mine."

Arlo walked over to Isadora and took her hand in his. The two were transported to the other side of the field as soon as he touched her hand. Arlo sat on the ground and ran his fingertips over the grass; the blades tickled his palm and released a harp sound upon each stroke. As the music echoed across the field, he looked at Isadora and smiled.

"They miss you, you know?"

Isadora smiled and fell back on her elbows. "Sometimes, I hear them calling out to me in the forest."

"Really?"

"Yeah. My father mostly, but sometimes I hear them both. They apologize for my suffering."

"What do you say to them?"

Isadora smiled again and remained silent.

Suddenly two puppies appeared at their feet. The playful pups tumbled over one another as if they were involved in a serious game. Isadora laughed when one of the puppies jumped on her leg and sprang across to Arlo's.

"Look at him! He's so cute!" said Isadora, rubbing the dog's head.

"Yeah, he's a feisty one," replied Arlo.

Suddenly two more puppies appeared at Arlo's feet and attempted to crawl up his leg, making him burst into laughter. He petted the dogs and turned to Isadora. "I think they see me sometimes."

"You do?"

"Now and then, I get the urge to look over my shoulder because I feel like they're watching."

"Have you told them how you feel?"

"All the time."

"I think they hear you. No . . . I'm sure of it."

Arlo reached out and touched Isadora's hand again. This time instead of transporting to another location, Isadora's brown eyes became so clear, Arlo could see all the emotion she had inside.

"I'm happy you're here with me, Isadora."

Isadora stared back at Arlo, her heart filled with passion. "I love you."

"I love you, too."

As the teenagers leaned over and kissed, a large group of puppies burst from the vegetation. While Arlo and Isadora kissed, the pack of dogs circled the area before coming back to jump on the unsuspecting kids, peppering their faces with wet tongues and cold noses.

"Ahhhhhh!" laughed Isadora, pulling Arlo close.

Arlo sat forward, scooped up a handful of puppies, and pushed them into his face—they smelled like bubblegum, and he couldn't get enough of their scent. Isadora sat up, laughing uncontrollably.

"Hey, Arlo," she said with a radiant smile.

"Hi, Isadora," replied Arlo.

The two teenagers stood and took off, running toward the waterfall with the dogs chasing closely behind.

22

The Strength of the Huturo

Carla wasn't feeling well. She had just picked up her children from school when nausea struck. As her sons played around in the back seat, Carl looked at her face in the mirror and was stunned—her eyes were puffy, and her skin was dark red.

"How was school today, boys?" she asked, trying to hide her illness.

"It was okay," replied Jude.

"Nothing new," Blake chimed in.

Carla cracked a weak smile. "Good because you know that . . ."

Suddenly the need to throw up overpowered Carla, and she quickly pulled over. She only had time to open the car door before a powerful stream of vomit shot out of her mouth.

"Mom, what's wrong?" asked Blake, unfastening his seatbelt.

Carla continued throwing up, waving her hand at her son to get back in his seat. After vomiting twice more, she finally sat up, grabbed a handful of napkins from the glove box, and wiped off the door.

"Don't worry, boys. I'm okay. Fasten your seat belts."

When Carla looked back at the road, she saw dozens of cars pulled over. Drivers were leaning out of their car windows, vomiting, while some were on their knees, throwing up uncontrollably.

"Mommy, what's going on?" asked Jude.

"I don't know, baby," replied Carla.

Carla turned on the radio.

"This just in to the One-Eight-Three-Nine-Three News Desk. A health emergency has been issued for Fairfax County and all surrounding areas. The police and local health authorities are asking everyone to shelter in their homes or businesses for the next forty-eight hours. We'll have more updates shortly."

Carla quickly turned off the radio. The last thing she needed was for her sons to be riled up by an emergency. Both had asthma, and neither was good at handling excitement. She pulled back onto the road but immediately stopped; she was in the middle of a traffic jam with dozens of cars unable to break free.

"Mom, I'm hungry," complained Blake. "Can we get burgers?"

Frustrated, Carla turned around. "I can do many things, Blake, but none involve lifting an SUV into the sky."

Suddenly a giant red webbed foot landed in the center of Carla's windshield, shattering the glass.

"AAAAAHHHH! MOMMY!" screamed the children, pointing at the window.

A red face appeared on the windshield, two enormous eyes peering into the car. The creature pressed its human nose against the cracked glass and sniffed, releasing a terrifying giggle as it captured the scent of the family. It looked deeply into Carla's eyes, searching for something inside her—emotion, fear, or something else. After a few seconds, the creature slammed its four arms against the glass, shattering it thoroughly before stepping onto the car's roof and moving on to the next vehicle.

Carla and her sons watched in horror as the creature smashed the car's windshield behind them and yanked the driver from the vehicle. With its spiderlike arms, it held the terrified man by his torso while the other two arms held the man's neck and head; in one powerful motion, it pulled the man's head off his body with the spinal cord attached, and let the torso slide down the hood of the car onto the street. The creature held up the man's head, seemingly celebrating the beheading of its victim, spinning in a circle, showing it for all to see. Suddenly the creature's body jerked, and its chest opened like the wings of a bird. It grabbed the dangling spinal cord of the dead man and inserted it into its chest. Soon the man's eyes were blinking, his eyes blood red, and a terrifying grimace on his face. In one motion, it retreated into the monster's chest cavity and the opening closed. The creature turned back to look at Carla, and released another terrifying scream before jumping onto the next vehicle.

Carla and her sons were silent, staring in disbelief at what was happening on the street. There were dozens of the creatures running through traffic, ripping open car doors and tearing people apart. Suddenly a machine gun sounded from behind, and Carla turned to see several men dressed in military uniforms firing shots at the monsters. The bullets hit two monsters beside her car. Still, they only seemed to be a minor annoyance—the creature's smaller arms fell to the ground, transforming into glowing red-winged scorpions that buzzed into the air and attacked the soldiers, ripping off pieces of their faces with their claws. The host of the scorpion arm stood in the center of traffic, breathing heavily as it watched the creature rip the soldier's body to shreds. Suddenly two thin, branch-like arms appeared, replacing the missing ones and, in seconds, were functional.

When the two monsters left, Carla saw her chance and gunned the car into traffic. Swerving around open car doors and running over corpses, she pushed the car as fast as possible. But suddenly, a voice came from behind her.

"Mom," whimpered Jude. "Blake."

Carla turned to see her son leaning to the side, clutching his arm; a bullet struck him in his shoulder, and he lost a lot of blood.

"Blake!" screamed Carla. "Mommy's coming!"

Carla stopped the SUV, climbed out of the car, and ran to the passenger side. Just as she was about to open the car door, she felt a great thrust inside her chest that lifted her off her feet. She landed on her back and screamed—something was inside her, pushing at her stomach to get out. In excruciating pain and vomiting blood, Carla tried grabbing for the door handle to reach Blake, but another thrust came from inside her, and she lost feeling in her legs. The thing inside her stomach shredded her and climbed out of Carla's body. It looked like a tiny red devil with enormous eyes and a human nose, a smaller version of the monster on the hood of her car but more terrifying.

"SOMEBODY! HELP ME!" screamed Carla.

The baby monster buried its face in Carla's stomach and pulled on something that sent a sharp pain directly to her heart. It was the worst feeling Carla had ever felt. The sensation was like someone had cut her chest open and was poking her heart with a rusty fork. Carla screamed —but nothing came out. The sound of the beast sucking her blood and chewing on her flesh was driving Carla insane. She couldn't take much more of the tearing and ripping. She lay on the side of the road, wanting it all to end, drifting in and out of consciousness as she watched the fantastical creature devouring her body right before her eyes.

The beast grew in size with each gulp of entrails, giggling like a child as it found more delicious pieces of her body to devour. Within seconds it was the size of one of Carla's children, all the while eating bigger bites of her stomach and intestines. Finally, the monster was the same size as the others and stood like a towering menace over her damaged body. With two hands, it grabbed Carla's neck and held her torso with the other two hands. The pull brought instant blackness to Carla's eyes—she didn't feel her head and spine separate from her body. The monster's chest opened, and it plugged her into its insides. Suddenly Carla could see again, her head swimming around the creature like the tentacles of an octopus, watching a new world covered in red. Her eyes fell on her children, terrorized in the car, crying, clutching one another as they watched their mother's transformation into something with evil intent. She felt nothing for those children. The wholeness of evil was all that mattered, and she was one with the creature that brought forth this world of pain. Seconds later, Carla was resting inside the creature's chest, waiting for a new kill.

23

Sisterhood

"Shit!"

Indigo came storming out of the bathroom and stood before her two sisters. "Okay, which one of you took a dump and didn't flush?"

Inez lowered her glasses and looked at her sister. "Not me. That's disgusting."

Both sisters glared at Penny until she paused the game. "My bad," Penny responded dryly.

Indigo shook her head, walked back into the bathroom, and flushed the toilet. "You're unbelievable. You're three hundred years old and behaving like an infant. It takes less than one second to press the handle!"

"Oh, stop your bellyaching, Indi. You act like you never made a mistake."

"I swear. I'm so tired of living with the two of you."

Inez closed her laptop. "You two always do this. You see that I'm working."

"Working? Since when?" yelled Indigo from the bathroom.

Penny snickered and restarted her video game. "She means searching the ads for a new boyfriend."

"Since when is finding a boyfriend a job?" chuckled Indigo.

Inez got up and went into the kitchen. "Since I live with two unsupportive sisters intent on making me single for all eternity."

Penny paused the game again. “That’s cap, Inez, and you know it. The last guy left because of your behavior.”

Indigo walked into the living room, rubbing lotion on her hands. “She’s got you on that one, Inez.”

Penny winked at her sister. “Damn right. You talked hella shit to Parker on the phone.”

“I did not!”

“I heard you! That sharp tongue gave him every reason to leave. Well . . . that plus that four-hundred-year-old cookie.”

Penny and Indigo burst into laughter. “Forget you, Penny. Cap? Is that another one of your slang words? Grow up already.”

“Yes, it’s slang—capping means lying. Catch up with the times and stop acting like an old sour puss from the 1800s. But I don’t know why you call me immature when you’re the one surfing the web for a date.”

Indigo flopped down on the sofa next to Penny. “Don’t worry, Inez. Dating is difficult for all of us. It’s hard to be in a relationship with a mortal with only forty good years.”

Penny put down her video game controller and gave Inez a peck on the cheek. “Yeah, sis, I’m just playing. We know it’s hard out there. How long have we been doing the hotel hook-up thing?”

“Since forever,” piped Indigo. “I don’t even bother anymore.”

“Me, either, “continued Penny. “Explaining why I can’t take someone home is a bitch! What am I supposed to say? ‘Hey, I live in a crystal house on the treetops of Blood Mountain.’ The first time I said that to a guy, he’d look at me like I was insane.”

“Yeah, that would certainly make them run—well, that plus your rotting hand,” quipped Inez.

Penny removed the glove from her hand and inspected it—the skin was green, and the nails on the fingers were still black.

“That fucking bitch!” she cursed. “But I think it’s getting better.”

“Jeez, that stinks!” complained Indigo, covering her nose. “You should go outside to air that thing out.”

Penny put on her glove, went into the kitchen, and removed the bag from the garbage can. “Be back in a sec,” she said.

Penny snapped her finger, and a green aura appeared around her body. She walked through the crystal wall and tumbled head over heels through the air until she landed on her feet on the ground.

“Shit. I forgot,” Penny said, remembering the rain they started.

Penny tossed the garbage into a pit, snapped her finger, and aimed, shooting a stream of fire from her index finger, igniting the trash. Penny heard fluttering on the opposite side of the clearing as she watched the flames burn the refuse.

“Hey, Indi!” Penny yelled up to her sister.

“Yeah!”

“You forgot to bring the laundry in out of the rain. Did you forget about the spell we cast?”

“Shit!”

“The clothes will smell like a dog’s ass for a week! Do you want me to grab them?”

“What kind of stupid question is that? Of course I want you to bring them in.”

“Ungrateful jerk,” Penny whispered.

She waved her hand, and the clothes flew off the line, folded, and landed in her palm. As she turned to fly back up to the house, she heard the deep growl of an animal in the bushes. Suddenly a flame appeared in Penny’s fist, and she slowly turned around.

“You may as well come out. There’s no sense in hiding.”

A large black wolf walked out from the shadows, raised fur glistening in the rain. Although the creature had a menacing growl and piercing eyes of fire, Penny remained calm. Without looking in the wolf’s direction, she sniffed the laundry as though the creature wasn’t there.

“Hi, Forneus. We’ve been expecting you.”

The growling wolf shook the water from its coat and moved closer.

There was a slightly noticeable breeze in the air, and Penny smiled. Her sisters were here.

"Hey, Forneus," said Inez from the opposite side of the clearing.

The beast turned in her direction, snarling and curling back its lips to show its sharp teeth.

"Stand when you speak to my sister," demanded Inez.

Inez clapped her hands together, and the wolf fell to the ground. As it lay incapacitated, a ghostly image of Forneus's skeleton, covered in fire, rose from the wolf and stood before them.

"I mean no disrespect," said Forneus.

Another voice rose from behind the skeleton.

"We know why you're here, so let's get this over with," said Indigo, stepping out from the shadows.

Penny tossed the stack of clothing into the air and waved her arm, sending the clothes flying into the house.

"You want us to help you start a war," said Penny.

Forneus's eyes moved from one sister to the other. "Not *start.* I need your help in protecting the innocent from being attacked."

Penny shrugged. "It makes no difference to us. We hate the boy and his bitch of a babysitter."

"So you know what they intend to do?"

Indigo chuckled. "Do we know? We helped them fortify their soldiers."

Forneus seemed confused. "You know the Demon Balam controls the boy, and still you offered assistance? They intend to kill millions, and you will be partially responsible for those deaths."

Inez became angry. "Don't come to us with that self-righteous I-want-to-save-the-world crap. You've been filling Hell with souls for years, gravedigger."

"But Hell tricked me!"

"Potato, potato. Either way, we know the punishment Heaven gave you."

Indigo moved closer to Forneus's image. "Look, let's not waste our time bickering. You don't like the boy, and neither do we. Let us improve our positions through a mutually beneficial collaboration."

"What do you suggest?"

"The rain."

Forneus looked around. "This is your doing? I knew it was attached to Hell somehow—the liquid is thick with the scent of evil."

Penny wiped the liquid from her arms. "Yeah, I hate it, too," she said.

Forneus was silent for a moment. "I want to resurrect the dead," he finally said.

Inez seemed confused. "Don't you already possess that power? You don't need us for that."

"I need much more than I could bring back alone."

Indigo looked at her sisters. "Balam's army will cover the city in two or three days, and within two or three months, they'll be everywhere," she explained to her sisters.

Penny shook her head in disagreement. "We cannot be responsible for resurrecting all the dead souls. Doing something like that would surely get the attention of Heaven, and I don't want that kind of smoke."

"Penny, the number of Huturo will be enormous. We have to do something."

"How about this," explained Inez. "For every Huturo created, we allow the resurrection of three souls."

Penny laughed. "A fucking three-for-one sale? Are you serious? What are we, a discount department store?"

Forneus and the other two sisters remained emotionless as they contemplated the agreement.

"It's an acceptable number," said Inez. "But the Huturo are powerful creatures, and the only power the dead possess is abnormal strength."

"Not to mention their need to feed," piped Indigo. "The undead will kill their fair share of innocents."

Forneus lowered his head to think. "It is a necessary evil I'm willing to accept. The Huturo will kill many more than the undead, and I have to do what I can to protect the innocent."

Penny laughed again. "Fuck, Forneus. That punishment from Heaven must be a serious bitch if you're contemplating this one."

Inez's mouth fell open, and she moved closer to Forneus, staring into his eyes. Finally, she turned to Penny. "Don't laugh, sis," whispered Inez. "Can't you see? He's doing it for love."

All three sisters suddenly grew silent, staring at Forneus in awe as he looked away into the dark, rainy forest.

"We will help you," said Indigo.

Forneus looked at the women. "Thank you. But there is something else. The boy under my tutelage, Arlo, should possess the power to command the undead."

Inez seemed surprised. "Are you sure about this? He's only a teenager with underdeveloped volatile emotions."

"It is what I request."

The three sisters huddled together, whispering. After a few moments, Inez turned to Forneus. "Anything else?"

Forneus shook his head.

"We will alter the rain spell without the boy's knowledge. Give us two days," Inez said.

"Thank you."

Penny's hand began glowing, and slowly Forneus's image melted into the wolf. After a few seconds, the wolf stood, shook the rain off, and turned toward the forest.

"Forneus!" yelled Inez.

The black wolf turned and looked back at the girls with glowing eyes.

"There is something you should know. Your boy's mother is alive and being held captive by John."

The wolf growled and nodded its head before disappearing into the dark forest.

Inez sighed. "That's so romantic. I wish I had a man that felt that way about me."

Penny agreed. "Yeah, men like him are hard to find."

Indigo shook her head. "Too bad he's not going to make it."

Inez wiped a tear from her eye. "We don't know that because we didn't see it in the bones. Still, Forneus's suffering will be tragic."

Penny wiped the rain off her face. “Come on. Let’s get out of this rain before the smell attaches to our hair.”

Penny waved her hand, and all three women disappeared.

24

Recalibration

While Isadora lay sleeping on the grass, Arlo sat looking at something peculiar across the field—he spotted a miniature orange tree. He hadn't noticed it before because of the numerous larger plants, but Arlo couldn't turn away after he saw it. It seemed so out of place amongst the other lush foliage that he wondered if someone had come into the garden and secretly planted it there. Unable to keep his curiosity at bay, Arlo pushed aside the sleeping puppies on his lap and walked over for a closer look.

The orange tree was a runt of a sapling, its trunk barely long enough to bend toward its portion of sunshine amongst the other tall plants. But it was still there, pushing, surviving despite other taller plants, reaching for what it needed. Its fruit was pathetic; the four tiny oranges with uneven coloring were no larger than a cherry. Arlo picked a fruit from the tree and inspected it; the orange's partially green skin was thin and burst in Arlo's hand, squirting juice everywhere. Arlo lifted his wet hand to his mouth and tasted the liquid.

"Disgusting," he whispered.

The fruit tasted like a combination of lemon juice and castor oil. Arlo wiped his tongue with the back of his hand, but the taste intensified, burning his nose like ammonia. Arlo grabbed a handful of grass and rubbed it on his tongue, but the flavor got worse, and he started to cough.

"Sometimes . . ." a voice whispered behind him.

Arlo turned around and saw his father standing before him. "Dad?" asked Arlo, dazed and confused.

Jamie smiled and touched his son's shoulder. "Sometimes the bitter taste is necessary."

"What do you mean?"

"No one moves to the life beyond without experiencing today's pain."

"Is that why you were mean to me?"

Jamie smiled. "Children are mirrors, and their young lives always reflect the successes and failures of their parents."

Arlo felt tears welling up from within. "That's not what I asked. Do you love me?"

Jamie lowered himself to his knees beside his son. "My love for you is eternal."

Tears streamed down Arlo's face, and he fell into his dad's arms. There was a rumbling in the sky, and they both looked up to see the sun flashing a million colors, leaving a trail of sparkles as it descended toward the horizon.

"It's almost time for you to go."

"But I don't want to. Where's mom? Can you bring her here?"

Jamie looked at Isadora sleeping on the grass with the puppies. "She is a good match for you."

Arlo turned to look at Isadora. "Yeah, she's great. Hey, remember that time she called the house? I thought you and . . ."

Arlo didn't get a chance to finish his sentence. When he looked up, his father was gone.

Arlo wiped his face and walked across the field to Isadora. She woke up as he pushed through the dozens of sleeping puppies on the ground.

"Hey," she said, making room for him.

"Hey."

"I spoke to my mom and dad."

"Really?"

"Yeah."

"What did they say?"

Isadora's eyes filled with tears. "They said they forgive me."

Arlo smiled and touched Isadora's face. "That's nice, Isadora."

"They also told me they like you."

Arlo looked surprised. "Me? You told them about me?"

"I didn't have to tell them anything because they knew about you from the moment we met."

Arlo tried to change the subject. "I saw my Dad."

"You did? What did he say?"

"He told me he loved me."

Isadora threw herself into Arlo's arms. "That's so wonderful, Arlo."

"Yeah, I know."

Arlo and Isadora looked up at the sun.

"We're almost out of time, I guess," Arlo said.

"Yeah. How do we get out of here?"

The couple turned to look behind them and saw a white building. When they turned back to face one another, their eyes met.

"Do you really love me, Arlo?"

Arlo moved in close. "I do love you, Isadora."

They kissed passionately, causing one of the dogs to wake up and stare at them. Isadora noticed the curious dog and pulled away.

"I think we have company," said Isadora, embarrassed.

Arlo laughed and lied down on the grass.

Soon Isadora lied down and snuggled close until Arlo wrapped his arm around her.

"You know, I'm probably going to die untouched."

Arlo flashed Isadora a curious look.

"What do you mean?"

Isadora smiled. "Never mind."

"No, Isadora. Tell me what you mean."

Isadora propped herself up on an elbow. "We've never . . . I mean, I've never *done* it."

"Done what?"

Finally, Arlo understood what she meant, and his eyes widened. "Oh, that."

Suddenly all the dogs' heads shot up, and they sprinted away, yapping loudly.

"Hey! Where are you going?" yelled Isadora.

Arlo looked at Isadora and shook his head. "I think they're trying to tell us something."

"What?"

"I don't think that kind of behavior is allowed here."

Isadora chuckled. "Yeah, this place is kind of sacred, huh?"

"Yeah."

Suddenly, a dog peeked out from the bushes as if it heard the teens acknowledge their misplaced emotions.

"Well, forget the virginity thing. Is it okay to hold one another while we sleep? Can we do that?" asked Isadora.

"Sure," replied Arlo, wrapping his arms around her.

Suddenly all the dogs rushed out of the bushes and jumped on them again. Isadora and Arlo played with them until the dogs were tired. Eventually, they all lied on the grass and fell asleep.

25

Trespassers

"Arlo! Get up!"

Arlo sat up, startled. The wind was blowing furiously, and the dogs were gone. Arlo looked up in the sky and saw thousands of demonic red eyes staring down at them. He looked to the horizon for the sun and saw it sinking quickly, almost gone.

"We slept too long!" yelled Arlo.

"Come on!" screamed Isadora. "We've got to get out of here!"

Isadora and Arlo sprinted toward the white building. As they ran, the wind blew them off their intended path, making them run harder to reach their destination. As they drew closer to the building, Arlo looked up and saw the evil eyes becoming larger, drawing closer to them as mighty thunder rumbled through the sky.

Isadora reached the door first, and she immediately pushed the door open and ran into the darkness. After being blown to the ground by a gust of wind, Arlo climbed to his feet. Just as he ran into the dark room, something enormous slammed against the door, sending Arlo and Isadora sliding across the room.

"What was that?" asked Isadora.

"I don't know," replied Arlo.

After sitting in the dark for several minutes, Arlo slid across the floor to Isadora. "What are we supposed to do?" he asked.

"Sleep, maybe?" replied Isadora. "After all, we won't get any sleep back home."

Arlo wrapped his arms around Isadora and squeezed her tight. "Let's catch a few Zs."

The teens closed their eyes and went to sleep.

26

Back to the Afterlife

Arlo blinked a few times and opened his eyes. He was back in the dark shack in the middle of the forest. After searching the room, he realized his arm was still inside Isadora's chest, clutching her heart. Arlo cautiously released his grasp of the muscle, and his arm slid out.

As he lay in silence on the floor, gathering his faculties, Arlo realized an immediate difference in his senses. Inside the Priming Fields, his body was just as it had been in high school. But now that he was back, he noticed significant changes. Along with diminished hearing in his left ear, an intermittent feeling in his chest came and went, alternating between excruciating pain and a freezing sensation, like ice cream sliding down his insides.

Arlo looked over at Isadora's body and saw her looking back at him with her mangled face, trying to figure out everything, just as he was. Isadora looked down, noticed her hand inside Arlo's chest cavity, and took it out.

"You okay?" her muffled voice asked inside Arlo's head.

Arlo attempted to speak. "Uhhhhhh," he moaned, forgetting his physical ability to verbally communicate no longer existed.

Arlo concentrated, and then he was able to speak with his mind. *"I forgot I couldn't speak. Yeah, I'm okay."*

Suddenly their senses opened, and the world came crashing in. There were voices everywhere, and it seemed like hundreds of people were trying to break into the building.

"I know you're in there," whispered an old scraggly female voice. "We can smell you."

"I'm going to rip your fucking head off and eat your tongue!" yelled a husky male voice.

Suddenly there came a tremendous pounding at the wall behind Isadora and Arlo, and they moved away.

"Please let us in. We just want to talk," yelled the soft voice of a young boy.

After a few moments, the pounding intensified, and the boy started yelling. "You don't understand," continued the boy. "I have to eat you. Please?"

Arlo and Isadora remained motionless, listening to the evil outside.

Finally, the boy spoke again. "You and your pretty bitch will never escape. We'll roast your guts over a campfire and feast on your liver."

Suddenly Arlo heard a growling nearby.

"Please! Get away! The two kids inside are mine!"

The creature moved closer until it finally attacked.

"Noooo! Stop! Mommy! Daddy! AHHHHHHH!"

Arlo and Isadora listened silently as the creature ripped the boy apart and ate him. When the animal finished, it began clawing at the wall, roaring louder and louder as it attempted to enter.

"There you are," mumbled a deep voice from the other side of the room.

Arlo and Isadora looked up to see Forneus standing in front of the stoned entrance, fortifying it with other rocks. They climbed to their feet and stumbled over to help him.

"What's happening? Is this because we're late?" asked Arlo.

"Maybe your emotions prevented you from heeding my warning, but I told you what would happen."

Isadora grabbed a small stone and handed it to the towering skeleton. *"Sorry, Forneus. We fell asleep."*

Suddenly a machine gun sounded outside the door.

"I'll get you sons of bitches," a southern-twanged voice yelled.

Arlo and Isadora moved away while Forneus continued working.

"How long is this going to go on?" asked Isadora.

"Now that you've returned, it'll probably be intense for a few more hours. By tomorrow we'll have one or two stragglers, but they'll mostly be gone."

Arlo remembered the fire and became worried. *"What about food?"*

Forneus motioned to the corner. *"Don't worry, boy. There are four dead pigs over in the corner. We'll be fine."*

After putting the final stone in place, Forneus sat in front of the door. *"How are the two of you feeling now?"*

Arlo and Isadora glanced at one another.

"We're a lot better," said Arlo. *"Stronger, too."*

Forneus couldn't smile with his skeleton face, but Arlo thought he saw one.

"The Priming Field does wonders for the spirit," Forneus said.

Suddenly a new voice rang out—a young woman. "Hey, Arlo. Please let me in. They're going to kill me out here."

Arlo's eyes widened, and he stood.

"You know her?" asked Isadora.

"I don't know. Maybe. That voice sounds familiar," replied Arlo.

Forneus extended his skeletal arm and blocked Arlo from the entrance.

"Down, boy. It's a trick to get us to open that door. It would be best to remember that all this activity is from overstaying your time in the Priming Field. Anyone outside that door is evil and wants to take you to Hell."

Arlo returned to Isadora's side and sat listening.

"Open the door, you fucking bastard! I'm going to cut your throat and send you to Hell!"

Arlo shook his head and closed his eyes. *"Jeez. These fucking people."*

Isadora turned to Forneus. *"Were you able to reach the women in the forest?"*

"Yes. The process will initiate in three days."

Arlo was confused. *"What process? What are you guys talking about?"*

Forneus chuckled. *"That's right. You were so deep in your self-pity that we didn't tell you. Those creatures you saw when you visited your parents are from Hell, and the only way we have to stop them from blanketing the world is by fighting them with the undead."*

"How many of them are there?"

"By now, there are thousands of them."

"But how can you fight them with the undead? Will the undead possess special powers or something?"

"No. Just teeth and bone. But that is all they need."

Arlo shook his head in disagreement. *"I saw those things. They have special powers that we don't. It'll be a slaughter."*

"We have one thing the creatures of Hell don't possess."

"What?"

"You."

"Me?"

"I haven't told you, but my visions show you as the key to their destruction."

"You're mistaken. I don't have special powers. Hell, I can't even talk."

"The women in the forest agreed to give you one special power—you will lead, and the undead will follow your commands."

"In a war against Hell? Are you crazy?"

"It is our only hope of stopping Hell's progression."

"And if I don't do it?"

"Then the people you knew in your younger days will die. They will send the children to Hell for enslavement, and their parents will be food for Hell's Army."

Arlo turned away. *"I didn't ask for this."*

Isadora grabbed Arlo's arm. *"Think about what Forneus is saying, Arlo. Our cousins, uncles, aunts, and friends will be killed or taken to Hell. How can we sit back and allow that to happen without fighting?"*

Arlo jerked his arm away from Isadora. *"What do you know about it? I would still be alive if it weren't for you!"*

Isadora lowered her head, and Arlo immediately regretted his words.

"I-I'm sorry, Isadora. I didn't mean . . ."

With her disfigured face, Isadora attempted a faint smile. *"It's okay, Arlo. I deserve that. You're right. You would still be alive if it weren't for me, and so would my family. But despite that truth, there's another—whether you were living or not, the monsters from Hell would still be here, and the outcome would be the same."*

The worms in Forneus's skull began screaming, lighting the room with their evil glow. *"What Isadora speaks is true. Death was your destiny, and whether you accept the task of trying to save the souls of the innocents is entirely your decision."*

Arlo looked from Isadora to Forneus. *"I need some time to think about it."*

Forneus rose from the floor, grabbed another stone, and piled it onto the others. *"There's one more thing to consider."*

"What's that?"

"Your mother."

Arlo's eyes widened. *"What about my mother?"*

"She's being held prisoner."

Arlo stared at Forneus in shock. *"Prisoner?! Where is she? I mean, how do I find her?"*

"She's being held captive by the one who took your life. You knew him as Manuel, but now he goes by John."

27

Come the Zombies Pt. 1

Starlight Cemetery

8:40 p.m.

"Shit! We've been busy as hell lately," complained Jasper.

"I know," replied Eric. "And that cheap fucker won't pay overtime."

Jasper lowered his shovel and rubbed his back. "That son of a bitch doesn't care that we're two old heads out here doing the work of four teenagers. He cares about getting that money."

"Hell, you know Jimmy doesn't care about two old fucks if he doesn't even care about his own soul. That bastard made me come in early last Sunday to unearth a couple of old graves and bury them on top of that youngster we buried last week."

"Piece of shit. Jimmy had me do the same thing to that lady that lost her little boy in that hit-and-run. Someone should dime his crooked ass out."

"Hell, I was this close to doing it a few months back, but Dorothy talked me out of it."

"Oh, yeah, Dorothy wouldn't allow you to do that. You have five kids."

Jasper took a deep drag of his cigar and looked into the sky before pulling down his hoodie.

"I've never seen rain like this, have you? It's thick, almost like yogurt."

Eric ran his fingers along his jacket and stared at his glistening hand. He lifted it to his nose and smelled it.

"This shit ain't rain. It's something else. It smells like chemicals."

Jasper smelled his hand. "It's sticky too. Global warming, maybe?"

"That's it. Pollution. These fuckers would sacrifice their mothers for a dollar. Let's finish this shit and go home."

Eric grunted in agreement, scooped up a pile of mud with his shovel, and tossed it into the grave. The soil landed in the hole with a splash. "If it continues raining like this, the graves won't keep."

Jasper angrily threw his cigar to the ground. "Fuck this."

Jasper stormed off to the far end of the cemetery and climbed onto the large backhoe parked underneath the shed. After attempting to start the vehicle several times, he grabbed a handful of wires beneath the dashboard, ripped a few open, and put several cables together, causing a spark. The construction vehicle roared within a few seconds, and Jasper drove it across the cemetery to the grave site.

"Hey!" yelled Eric. "You sure you want to do this? Jimmy's going to be mad."

Jasper revved the engine and scooped up a massive mound of muddy dirt. "Fuck him! I'm not staying out here all night in the rain."

After dropping the dirt on the grave, Jasper walked over to pat it down with his foot. As soon as he stepped on the grave, the mud shifted, and his foot sank. Jasper tried pulling his foot out, but only his sock-covered foot emerged.

"Oh, shit!" said Eric, doubling over with laughter.

"Goddamnit!" cursed Jasper.

Jasper balanced himself on one foot and reached down to retrieve his boot. As soon as he grabbed it, something pulled the shoe deeper into the mud, causing Jasper to land headfirst in the soil. Eric saw his friend's head buried deep in the mud, and crashed to the ground laughing uncontrollably.

"HAHAHAHAHAHA!" laughed Eric.

Jasper's arms pushed against the ground in an attempt to pull his head out of the grave. The sight of his friend's struggle caused Eric to laugh harder, and he could barely catch his breath. Suddenly Jasper's arms went limp, and his body collapsed on the ground, trembling.

"Hey, Jasper! You okay?" asked Eric.

Eric ran to the grave, grabbed Jasper around the waist, and tried lifting his friend out. As soon as he pulled on the body, Jasper began shaking violently and slipped out of Eric's hands. Terrified that his friend was suffocating, Eric grabbed Jasper again and pulled with all his might.

"Come on!" Eric screamed, struggling to get Jasper free.

Something jerked on Jasper's body, and he disappeared entirely underground. The mud began bubbling furiously, and Eric fell on his back.

"Oh my God!" whispered Eric, climbing to his feet.

Eric pulled out his cell phone and dialed 911.

"Yeah, I'm at the Starlight Cemetery on Benning Road. There's been an accident, and my friend is hurt. Send someone fast!"

Eric hung up, grabbed the shovel, and dug into the earth. As soon as the shovel touched the grave, something pulled it into the ground.

"Jasper, is that you?"

Fearing Jasper was running out of air, Eric ran to the backhoe and climbed onboard.

"I'm coming, Jasper. Hang on!"

Hot-wiring the engine, Eric dug a hole near the grave's edge and waited for the soil to pour out.

"Hey, Jasper! Push the dirt! Push your way out!"

But there was no movement.

A flash of lightning lit up the night, and the clouds exploded in a torrential downpour, drenching Eric as he waited for his friend to appear. But nothing came. Eric was panicking, so he climbed off the backhoe and prepared to run for help. He was about to run when he froze; in the distance, there were dozens of shadows in the cold, rainy darkness.

Eric moved toward them, waving his hands. "Hey! He's over here!" he yelled, beckoning for the shadows to come.

But the figures stood motionless, swaying back and forth in the storm. Suddenly another bolt of lightning struck, and Eric froze—the shadows weren't the police or emergency workers. They were corpses! The heavy rain clung to their muddy skin in an oily sheen, making the flesh on their faces hang from their skulls like ragged clothing. Some corpses were so old they were only skeletons with thin silver hair hanging from their heads. But all were dead, a strange green glow emitting from their eye sockets.

Lightning struck again, and Eric saw two familiar faces standing in the group.

Bobby Reynolds and Richard Stevens, Eric mouthed without realizing it.

He knew they were dead because he'd embalmed the two boys earlier that week. Eric remembered their family in the office making funeral arrangements, full of hysterics and crying while cursing the coward who caused their premature deaths. Eric remembered how he had carefully drained their blood and pumped them full of formaldehyde until their skin grayed.

"Oh my God!" Eric whispered.

As if reacting to the sound of the voice, the creatures broke into a frantic sprint, shrieking wildly, their milky white eyes focused on the man standing in the center of the cemetery. Eric turned to run but stumbled—the ground was opening around him with dozens of rotting hands pushing up through the mud. Eric jumped over the corpses' hands and landed near a partially buried skeleton halfway out of the ground. The monster saw Eric and screamed, slamming its face into Eric's shoe. But the creature's old teeth didn't penetrate, and Eric met its head with a vicious kick that shattered its skull, sending pieces of bone flying into the wet grass.

Eric tore through the cemetery, leaping over exploding headstones, and dodging zombies as they lunged at him. He reached the maintenance shed and darted inside—the truck he used to move items to different parts of the cemetery was his only way to escape. Eric opened the door and jumped inside.

"Come on . . . Come on . . ." Eric whispered as he searched for the keys.

When Eric lowered the visor, the keys landed in his lap. He frantically put the key in the ignition and turned it. Just as he did, he felt a searing pain in his midsection.

"AHHHHHH!"

Eric looked down and saw a dead baby chewing through his stomach. In an instant, he remembered where the Demon baby came from; on their boss's orders, Eric and Jasper had dug up the baby and left it on the lawn so they could add it into the same plot as another child.

Eric tried to push the demonic baby away, but its teeth were like razors, chewing voraciously into his stomach, tearing off his flesh, and sucking blood. Suddenly the windshield exploded, and shards of glass shot into Eric's face. One of the pieces stuck in Eric's eyeball, and he screamed in agony.

"Jesus Christ!" he roared.

With one hand, Eric tried fighting off the skeleton; with the other, he tried to pull the glass out of his eye. Soon the car began shaking back and forth; the other zombies had arrived and started jumping on the hood and crowding into the cabin.

"Please, Lord," Eric cried, "take my soul."

Eric began screaming again. One of the zombies opened a wound in the base of his neck, stuck its fingers in, and yanked upward, ripping off the top of Eric's head. His brain was exposed for only a millisecond before the zombies yanked out chunks of it and ate them. Eric never felt the corpses rip open his chest. By the time they ate his heart, he was long gone.

When the creatures finished eating, they returned to their moaning. They exited the maintenance shed and drifted mindlessly across the cold, wet cemetery.

Suddenly all the zombies paused and looked up into the rainy sky. After staring for several minutes, the corpses began moving away from the cemetery—toward the forest.

28

Come the Zombies Pt. 2

Greenlight Gas Station

9:30 p.m.

"Hey, Dion!"

"What?"

"Get me some candy and a soda!"

Dion paused and frowned. "You got some motherfucking money?"

Reggie pointed toward the gas pump. "I'm paying for the petro, ain't I? The least you can do is hook me up with a snack."

"Fuck you."

Reggie continued pumping gas and listening to the blaring car radio. After filling the tank, he put back the pump hose and walked around to the driver's side of the car. He was about to climb into the vehicle when he spotted something running down the street in his direction. Reggie closed the car door and stepped out to the edge of the gas station to get a better look. Suddenly three large deer ran past him and disappeared into the darkness.

"Fucking deer," mumbled Reggie, shaking his head. "They'll probably end up on someone's bumper tonight."

Reggie was about to climb into the car when he heard the click-clack sound of more hooves on the pavement. Suddenly a whole herd of deer came running past.

"Holy shit!" exclaimed Reggie.

When the group of deer was gone, Reggie stepped into the street to get a better look.

"Hey, dumb fuck! Get out of the street before you get hit by a car," yelled Dion as he exited the store.

"Yo! You'll never believe this. Come here!"

Dion walked over to his friend, stuffing his mouth from an open bag of chips. "What is it?"

"I don't know. Something's off."

"You mean like your brain?"

Reggie frowned. "I'm serious, dude. Something's going on."

Dion looked down the street and then turned back to the car. "I don't see shit, dude. Come on, let's get out of here. You know how Christina gets."

Reluctantly, Reggie walked over to the car and climbed inside. "Dude, Christina has got you whipped."

"Whipped?"

"Yep. Remember that . . ."

Reggie and Dion looked at one another—they could feel the ground rumbling beneath them. As they were about to climb out of the car, hundreds of animals ran past them.

"Holy fuck!" yelled Dion.

The two climbed out and stared in awe at the herd of animals that ran past them.

"What's going on?" asked Reggie.

Dion was worried. He dropped his bag of chips and climbed back into the car. "Come on. Let's get out of here."

Reggie agreed. He climbed in the car, revved the engine, and peeled out of the gas station parking lot onto the main road.

"What the hell are you doing?" asked Dion. "Didn't you see the animals going in the opposite direction?"

"Hold your horses!" yelled Reggie as he attempted to make a U-turn. But as he put the car in reverse to turn it around, he saw something at the end of the street. "Holy shit!"

There were hundreds of zombies sprinting toward them.

"Get us the fuck out of here!" screamed Dion.

Reggie whipped the car around and pressed the pedal to the floor. The vehicle fishtailed and crashed into a row of cars parked on the side of the street.

"What the hell are you doing?" yelled Dion angrily. "Get us out of here!"

Reggie tried to start the car, but it wouldn't turn on. The zombies jumped on the car, slamming their decaying heads into the windshield, trying to push through. One of the creatures locked eyes with Reggie. With thick green fluid pouring from its mouth and eyes, it cried out to the teenagers.

"Neeeeeed . . . brains."

Reggie stood transfixed. He couldn't take his eyes off the dead man trying to push his head through the windshield. The corpse looked like something out of a nightmare: a ghoul from Hell with searing green eyes, crawling through the torrential rain to eat him.

"Reggie!" yelled Dion, pushing against the wall of dead faces attempting to enter the car.

But Reggie didn't move—he couldn't; Reggie was like a deer trapped in headlights, afraid yet not quite believing what he was witnessing. Everything was moving around him in a blur; dozens of cold, wet hands slapped his face, scratched his skin, and filled the car with the stench of Hell.

Dion broke free of the zombies, opened the car door, and fell on the street. He quickly jumped up and took off, running back to the gas station.

"Dion!" screamed Reggie. "Don't leave me, bro! Help!"

Reggie watched as his best friend entered the gas station and locked the door. He tried fighting, but there were too many of them. A decrepit zombie bit off three of his fingers while another bit into Reggie's neck, spraying blood all over the car. But still, Reggie continued fighting. The zombies poured into the car on the passenger side, lunging for his head. With his injured hand, he made a fist, hit several of the creatures, and sent them sprawling onto the street. But there were just too many of them. Like an enormous blanket, they all jumped into the car and attacked. Reggie could do nothing but close his eyes.

Dion stared at the car rocking back and forth in the middle of the street, and turned around to face the small group of people huddled in the gas station. His best friend, Reggie, was gone, and he had abandoned him. Dion told himself he didn't have a choice, but he knew the truth—Dion had heard Reggie's cries for help as he sprinted away but chose not to look back.

Through the years, Reggie had been there for Dion on numerous occasions: when those guys jumped him outside the movie theater, Reggie was there; when Deon's girlfriend's ex had paid a group of guys to hurt him, it was Reggie who stood toe-to-toe against the gang, knuckled up and heart full of courage. Indeed, Reggie was ride or die. But when the time came for Dion to repay the courage his best friend showed for him, all Dion could do was run like a bitch. He could've grabbed a pipe, a mop, a tire iron from someone's car, anything to assist his friend. But Dion had chosen the easy road—the way of a coward.

Dion's eyes met with one of the customers, an elderly lady standing closest to him. He felt like she could see his cowardice; his blatant betrayal was so apparent, it looked like neon paint on his face. The old woman forced a small smile and continued staring at the zombie attack on the car. Dion felt anger at the lady. To him, the smile was a smirk, an intentionally intimate mockery that said: "I saw how you abandoned your friend, you coward son of a bitch."

Suddenly the lights went out, and one of the customers inside the gas station screamed.

"Shhhhh," whispered the cashier. "If those things see us, we're dead!"

The young boy moved close to Dion and touched his arm. "Sir, you wanna move to the back of the store with the rest of us? They might see you."

Dion sucked his teeth in frustration and ignored the boy. "My friend's out there. I'm not moving."

The clerk looked at the anger in Dion's eyes and left him to join the group.

"Hey!" exclaimed one of the men by the soda machines. "What are they doing?"

Dion ran to the window and saw the crowd of zombies stumbling around, staring at the sky.

"Why are they looking up?" asked the old lady.

Dion unlocked the door.

"Hey! What are you doing?" asked a teenage girl farthest from the door.

Dion ignored her and walked outside.

"Forget him!" yelled the clerk. "I'm locking it."

Dion heard the door lock behind him, but he didn't care. The zombies were walking into the forest on the other side of the street. Dion took a deep breath and walked over to Reggie's car. When he opened the door, he expected to see his best friend's mangled corpse drenched in blood. But instead, what he saw was an empty car. Dion walked to the other side of the vehicle and inspected further. Slowly he turned around and looked into the dark, rainy forest.

"Reggie is a zombie."

29

The Warrior

Arlo sat in the dark room, listening to the activity outside the building. The evil that he and Isadora awakened with their visit to the Priming Fields was gone. Now there was a new sound echoing through the forest, moaning and groaning that Arlo was intimately familiar with—the sound of the undead. They had been gathering outside the building for a few hours—first only a few stragglers and then, gradually, many more. Their cries of interrupted sleep were a song Arlo used to sing; the pains of his rotting body tortured him incessantly as he struggled to find his way.

As he sat in the dark listening, Arlo could tell some zombies were new to the undead world and struggling to navigate their strange existence. He heard people crying, the stutters to form coherent words, the thick sound of death stuck in their vocal cords. In contrast, Arlo also heard experience moving amongst the zombies; some were so old they assimilated the violence and agony by attacking the animals in the forest without instruction. They seemed happy to be able to move without the weight of cemetery soil pressing down on them, holding them captive in their coffins. The life of the undead was like clothing to them; they wore it naturally without questioning or fear.

Arlo could also hear the anti-undead mingling outside his door; they knew what death was and what it was not: an experience gained by clinging to their previous lives, worlds in which they could no longer participate. Arlo could hear the Sun Oil burning them without mercy, reducing them to crying, then cursing, and finally, a reduction to silence as the Sun Oil consumed them like a forest fire. Arlo envied these individuals the most; they had the courage he did not. No one had to tell them this level of existence was an abomination cursed by Heaven and Hell; they knew and wanted no part of it.

Towering over all the screaming, growling, and crying was Forneus's deep, gravelly voice. He'd sat inside with Arlo, listening to the gathering of the zombies until the ruckus became too loud. Fearing the Huturo would surely hear the noise and be drawn to it, Forneus had to go outside to insert calm into the mayhem. Arlo could hear Forneus moving amongst the group, coaching them, warning them. The tall skeleton had probably given the same pep talk to millions of souls before, just before he unknowingly delivered them into the arms of Hell. Still, the reluctant General Forneus sounded energetic and forceful, as if his own life depended on the success of the weakest individual. He empathized, pushed, and taught like a born teacher.

Suddenly the rock at the entrance slid aside.

"Arlo?" asked Isadora, peeking into the room. "Forneus wants you."

Arlo stood and walked out of the entrance into the rain. Thousands of zombies stared at Arlo with their green eyes as he made his way to the group's center. The scent of death was so thick, it rose like a great fog in the night. The zombies watched Arlo cautiously as if they recognized him as their leader but were doubtful of his intentions. Standing in the center of the group was Forneus, his skull of screaming worms casting an eerie glow on the faces of the dead.

"This is your army," said Forneus.

Arlo looked around in disbelief. "My army?"

"They will help you save your mother."

Arlo shook his head and cracked a smile. "You mean they will help *us*? You want to use them to help reunite you with your family, too, right?"

Arlo could tell Forneus didn't like his words, but the truth was the truth, and Arlo didn't like Forneus trying to make everything about his family. Something bothered him about Forneus's desire to avoid accepting responsibility.

Arlo looked around the group of rotting corpses before turning to Forneus. "How can I control them?"

"I don't know the mechanism used to move the undead. You will need to discover that for yourself."

Arlo turned to face an overweight bald man, half his brain rotting. After imagining the man attacking a nearby tree, the zombie suddenly roared, ran to the tree, and started punching the tree trunk continuously, leaving bloody stains on the bark. Arlo turned to another zombie, a little boy with black liquid oozing from his mouth. An image flashed in Arlo's mind, and the child became a growling, uncontrollable monster within a millisecond. He rushed to the fat zombie and slashed the man's face with his fingernails. When the man stumbled back, the child grabbed his chubby leg and tossed him far into the weeds.

Arlo turned to Forneus. "This might work."

Arlo walked through the other zombies, inspecting them, while Forneus walked closely behind. Finally, he arrived at a tiny skeleton barely able to stand. Arlo guessed it was a child, possibly a boy, dead for many years. Its long hair clung to its skull, while its bones were degraded, filled with holes like a sponge cake.

"Do you trust this puny skeleton to fight?"

Forneus looked down at the tiny skeleton, and the snakes inside his chest lit up. "Every soldier plays a part. Do not diminish their capabilities based on your idea of what a soldier should be. Our goal is to rid the world of the Huturo, and we should use every fist to help accomplish that."

"Maybe, but I've seen the Huturo. This tiny skeleton will only last a second."

"What do you suggest?"

"Let's stagger our attacks with the weakest out front. Their mobility is limited, and their bones are frail. Let's use them to draw the Huturo out."

"Agreed."

Isadora moved through the crowd of zombies to Arlo's side. "Does John even know you're alive?" she asked. "The last thing I remember is that he thought you were dead in the caverns of Black Forest."

Arlo's eyes lit up. "You're right. John doesn't know," replied Arlo.

The snakes in Forneus's chest began scurrying, illuminating the forest. Arlo could tell the news excited him.

"Excellent. If John believes you're dead, this gives us the element of surprise. We'll keep your presence hidden as long as possible. You and Isadora should monitor the attack from the shadows. For now, it's best to see how successful these souls will be in attacking the Huturo. Hopefully, we'll find a weakness and exploit it. For now, let's give these soldiers some practice by surrounding the city and attacking all the Huturo within the city limits."

"Where will you be?"

"I'll do my best to track down John. There's a good chance he's still in the children's hospital, but with so many of the Huturo ravaging the city, I don't know. John probably has your mother nearby with a lot of Huturo protecting them. It's best if we don't attack immediately. If he realizes our plan, John will kill your mother and call for reinforcements from Hell. I'm not sure we can handle that. We must thin the Huturo's numbers before we rush John's position."

Soon Arlo heard the wings of something enormous flying above them. He looked up and saw a colossal crow circling the group. The bird passed over the group of zombies and landed safely atop the building. After shaking the heavy rain from its wings, it tilted its head and stared at the zombies. Seemingly filled with disdain, it crowed again, its cawing sounding like laughter.

"Let's meet back here at sunrise," said Forneus.

Forneus walked to the building entrance, sat down on a stone, and leaned against the wall. The worms and snakes in his body lit up, and Forneus lowered his head. Soon the creatures in his body became stone, and the light dimmed until Forneus collapsed into a heap of bones. Arlo looked up at the bird and saw its eyes blazing with fire. The creature spread its enormous wings, rose in the rainy sky, and turned toward the city.

Arlo grabbed Isadora's hand. "Stay close to me."

Isadora chuckled, her laughter sounding like an old engine. "You stay close to *me*," she replied.

As Arlo and Isadora moved through the forest toward the city, the skeletons gathered in groups while the recently deceased fell to the back. After organizing themselves, the group of brooding monsters broke into a sprint toward the city.

30

The Lesson

People were running through the mall, terrified and screaming, with dozens of Huturo in pursuit. An overweight woman, scared and out of breath, wasn't keeping in step with the mob of people and fell.

"Please! Someone help!" she cried.

Before she could climb to her feet, she was pushed down again and crushed underneath the weight of the fleeing mob. It was pandemonium in the mall as the lights flashed off and on; the ground trembled as the mass of people pushed their way through stores, over benches, trampling any stationary person in their path. They could hear the demonic laughter of their pursuers rising amongst the madness, taunting them, terrifying them.

A teenager looked back into the rushing crowd for his friend but couldn't find him. They'd come to the food court together to grab a slice of pizza before going to the movies. Sure, there had been rumors floating around the school—strange things that happened to a classmate over the weekend, whispers of an unknown plague that made his classmate's family sick—but he never listened to rumors, especially if he didn't know the person. He and his friends chose to ignore it, chalking it up as another weapon adults used to keep kids from having fun. The boy and his friend both heard the news on the radio about sheltering in place but figured someone had their wires mixed up since the mall was still open. Now his friend was gone, lost in the scramble of the crowd.

The teenager looked back, trying to pick out his friend's face amongst the group. Still, the only thing he saw was the occasional red-faced monster rise from behind, eyes wide, cackling, the horrific screams of a victim, and then the mist of blood rising above the group.

The Huturo monsters were the definition of evil. They snatched victims randomly, tearing off their heads, and ripping out their spinal cords. They threw the remaining torsos ahead into the fleeing group, reveling in the screams of the terrified victims as chunks of flesh fell on their heads, spraying them with blood and feces.

"Daddy!" screamed a little girl.

Her father had been pulling her through the crowd when her hand slipped away. Now she was on the ground amongst the rush of hundreds of people trying to escape. Suddenly a Huturo spotted the child. With a gleeful shriek, it ripped apart a man standing nearby, shoved his head and spine inside its chest, and scooped up the little girl from the ground.

"AAAAAAAHHHHH! DADDY!" the child screamed.

The father saw the Huturo dangling the child in the air and rushed forward. The creature taunted the man by running one of its long fingers underneath the child's neck, mimicking a knife slicing the child's throat.

"Sarah!" the man yelled. "Don't worry! Daddy's coming!"

The man pushed over several people and slid on the blood-covered floor, crashing against a railing. He immediately regained his footing and sped toward his daughter, knocking over an elderly gentleman. Finally, when he was only a few feet away, he dove for her foot, grazing it with his hand before falling again. The Huturo cackled at the man's folly and dropped the girl to the ground. Its long spiderlike fingers grabbed the man and ripped his body apart. The child sat on the floor, trembling and whispering in disbelief at what she saw. The Huturo's chest opened like a butterfly, plugging in the spinal cord dangling from her father's head as the child watched, unable to speak. Soon her father's face, frozen in an excruciating expression, came back to life, now with a more sinister look, eyes filled with blood. The Huturo and her father turned to her and smiled before bounding into the group to grab another victim.

The terrified crowd exited the mall, everyone screaming and scattering into the flooded streets. The light rain was now a torrential storm, winds whipping wildly and water puddling the sidewalk. But there were even more of the Huturo outside. Dozens of the creatures splashed through the water, their red skin glistening in the darkness. The monsters enjoyed ripping apart the crowd like a buzzsaw from Hell, decapitating the fleeing and plugging them into their bodies before tearing bodies and tossing the corpses aside.

A Huturo grabbed a middle-aged woman and was about to rip her head off when she became angry and decided to fight back. The woman bit into the Huturo's finger, and black blood sprayed her face. The Huturo fell back in surprise and inspected its hand, glaring at the woman. Suddenly the woman fell to the ground and began screaming—she didn't realize the Huturo's blood had scorpions inside, and the tiny creatures scurried across her face and into her hair, pinching and biting.

The Huturo monster, still angry from the bite the woman delivered, turned to retreat but stopped. A group of soldiers was standing behind it, guns aimed.

"Fire!"

The soldiers shot the Huturo in the chest, and it cried out, alerting several monsters nearby. The creatures, furious at witnessing the attack, grabbed a nearby victim, ripped his head off, and tossed the torso into the group, sending the soldiers sprawling. As the Huturo stood holding the man's head, it suddenly dropped it to the ground and rushed its attackers with wide, blood-filled eyes. The Huturo's jawbone disconnected, opened its mouth wide, and bit one of the soldier's heads off. Releasing a bloodcurdling scream, the monster slammed its arms to the ground, and the arms detached, transforming into an enormous scorpion. The arachnid rushed the men, but they shot it before it was close, and it exploded.

"Help!" one of the soldiers screamed.

The other men turned to see two Huturo standing behind them, each with a soldier in their grasp. When they tried firing on the monsters, the Huturo jumped in the air, ripped the heads off the soldiers, and put them inside their open chests.

"Jenny!" yelled a woman through the mayhem.

Jenny turned to see her best friend, Laurie, standing on the other side of the street. "This way!"

Jenny darted between two Huturo and into a large group of fleeing people. After arriving at an abandoned car, she fell to the ground, slid underneath the vehicle, and came out on the other side. She quickly removed several scorpions hanging onto her blonde hair and sprinted to Laurie.

"How do we get out of here?" asked Laurie, tears streaming down her face. But Jenny had no time for tears—her whole body was teaming with adrenaline. After searching around frantically, she spotted their exit.

"There!" said Jenny, pointing to the forest just beyond a few small buildings.

She grabbed Laurie's hand, and the two women jumped over several torsos and slid underneath another car. When they stood up, they were in front of a pawnshop. Without hesitating, Jenny grabbed a brick from the ground and hurled it into the glass door. They ran into the shop, past the owner and his family huddling in the back, and out the backdoor.

"There!" said Jenny pointing to a linked fence at the edge of the parking lot. The women ran to the fence and were about to climb when they heard a loud noise behind them.

"Jenny!" yelled Laurie.

They turned around to see two Huturo burst out of the building, holding the owner's and his wife's heads in their hands. The creatures saw Jenny and Laurie, shoved the victims' heads into their chests, and ran toward the women.

Laurie landed on the other side of the fence first and turned to help Jenny. Just as she did, Laurie felt something sharp on her head. Suddenly blood was everywhere—in her eyes, her face, and pouring down the front of her shirt.

"Jenny," Laurie said weakly. "I'm hurt."

Jenny was about to land on the ground when she stopped and hurried back to the top of the fence; a skeleton with thin gray hair had bitten into Laurie's scalp while another had its arm inside her stomach, tugging at her organs. Jenny looked around, terrified—hundreds of skeletons and zombies were running out of the forest toward her. Jenny quickly looked back at the pawnshop and saw the building explode as dozens of Huturo burst out, sprinting toward her.

"Shit," whispered Jenny.

Jenny fell from the fence and sat on the ground to await her demise.

But something strange happened.

The Huturo saw the zombies sprinting out of the woods and stopped. The monsters tilted their heads in curiosity, unsure what to make of the army of undead monsters racing toward them. As the zombies grew closer, the Huturo registered a visible panic, flashing panicked looks amongst themselves, trying to figure out their response.

Three skeletons arrived at the first Huturo and jumped on it viciously. Without hesitating, one bit into its head, peeling back the crimson skin with its teeth, trying to reach the sweet brain inside the Huturo's skull. As the creature drank the venomous black blood of the monster, the zombie ignored the hundreds of tiny scorpions shooting down its throat. The other two skeletons bit the Huturo's chest with ravenous ferocity, their green eyes burning brighter at the sight of blood. The Huturo attempted to fight them off, but the skeletons were too mindless, too hungry. A strange metallic noise came from deep inside the Huturo as it seemingly registered damage to itself. The creature tried to push one zombie skeleton off, but the other undead bit off two of its fingers, sending scorpion-filled blood spraying everywhere. With their old teeth, the zombies continued tearing into the Huturo, sucking the arachnid-laced blood leaking from its skull, trying to get at the brain.

Finally, the Huturo flung the attackers away, and its chest flew open, filling the air with the smell of rotting meat. The three human heads inside the creature's chest cavity shot out and began flailing wildly like the tentacles of an agitated octopus. The faces on the end of the spinal cords were wrinkled and twisted with anger.

"Yooooooou," they hissed. "We will kill yoooou."

Suddenly the Huturo's body became erect, and all the crimson color in its skin changed to dark gray. With its chest open and the life drained from its body, it fell to the ground. The three flailing skulls stopped moving, and their spinal cords stiffened, making them stand upright in the Huturo's corpse, like a totem pole. Slowly, the skulls melted and dripped down the spinal cords into the dead Huturo, filling it with a strange green liquid. The other Huturo saw the damage to the other creature and began crying like children. They made angry, vengeful faces at the zombies before leaping over the destroyed building to continue chasing victims on the other side.

Arlo and Isadora stepped into the light. They'd been watching the Huturo from the shadows, intentionally holding most of their zombie army back while they searched for a weakness in the Huturo.

"Come on," said Isadora. *"Let's check it out."*

Arlo quickly pulled her back into the shadows. *"Wait. Something's happening."*

A strange violet mist was leaking out of the Huturo's body. Arlo's eyes immediately fell on Jenny, the girl who somehow managed to evade the attention of both the Huturo and the zombies. She laid flat on the ground, tucked tight against the fence, hoping all the monsters would overlook her presence. Her strategy had worked, but now the mist was drifting close, forcing her to try to cover her face. Although she buried her face in her jacket, the fog still got inside her, and she began convulsing violently on the ground. The other zombies noticed and sprinted toward Jenny, but they stopped when she lifted her head. Jenny's face was a throbbing mess of dozens of suctioning mouths puckering and sucking the air in search of food. Two large horns tore through her forehead, and her eyes were mouths with teeth, biting and sucking. Soon huge muscles bubbled beneath her skin, ripping off her clothes to reveal a body filled with the same deformity as her face—hundreds of mouths, all puckering and sucking for food.

Arlo was too preoccupied to remember to instruct the few nearby skeleton zombies to stay away from the creature. Two ran toward the monster, hoping to feast on its enormous mouth-covered head. As soon as they were close, the beast reached out with its massive arm and grabbed the skeleton. As it thrashed back and forth within the creature's grasp, the monster held it close to its face, relishing the meal to come, each of the mouths on its skin making loud slurping noises. After a few seconds, the creature locked the skeleton in a tight embrace against its body and held it firmly. Although the zombie was only bones, all the mouths on the monster sucked loud and hard until the zombie began to diminish, growing skinnier and smaller until, finally, there was only dust.

"A vampire from Hell," whispered Isadora.

Arlo nodded his head in agreement. *"That's what it is."*

But there was something more disturbing about what Arlo was witnessing. At the vampiric monster's feet, a strange purple vine spread rapidly, multiplying across the ground. As soon as the vine touched the fence, the barrier melted. But the vines didn't stop there. They crawled into the forest through the grass and the trees, killing everything they touched. Arlo looked at the dead Huturo lying on the ground, and saw the same purple vines crawling out of the body. The weed raced across the parking lot, making the asphalt bubble and melt before moving toward the building.

"Come on," said Arlo, grabbing Isadora's hand. *"We need to meet up with Forneus. Now."*

Arlo and Isadora ran into the forest, leaving the monster alone in the rain, sucking at the air in search of a new victim.

31

The Unknown Anger

John stood on the stairs of the hospital with the Witch Asura by his side, staring out into the stormy field. The light rain was now a storm, blowing violent gusts of wind and raining so hard, puddles were forming in the yard.

Hundreds of children stood on one side of the field encircled by a large wire fence. Some drifted to the location after their parents became Huturo, transformed by the virus the children unknowingly passed along. Others were drawn to the area after John visited them in their dreams, turning them into mindless shells of themselves. They all stood silently in the rain, unaffected by the relentless barrage of stinging water and wind gusts.

On the other side of the field were hundreds of Huturo. They roamed the yard, pushing past one another, stomping in the mud, and gleefully laughing as more monsters showed up every hour. John smiled as he watched them, all traces of their fragility erased by the rain. He could feel their desire to kill growing, building like a thunderous explosion in the clouds. John knew that soon the Huturo would be unstoppable.

"John?" asked Asura. "Is everything okay?"

John smiled. "More than okay. Things are progressing just as my Lord said they would."

"Will you enter the room to make physical contact again?"

"No. The rejuvenation process is too time-consuming. I'll deliver a progress report through mental contact."

"When?"

"Now."

Asura stepped back and closed her eyes. Soon John's body began trembling, and thick white foam poured from his mouth. A loud cracking noise sounded, and John's head spun around, his eyes black and oozing liquid. With his head facing backward, his body crumpled and fell to the floor.

"Who dares to interrupt?" whispered a voice in John's head.

John opened his eyes and looked around: everything was gone, and there was only blackness—only him standing in a dark place where light didn't exist.

"Lord Balam, it is John, your humble servant."

There was a pause, and then the deep, evil voice boomed. "YOU HAVE FAILED!"

"My Lord, I don't understand. I've done as you instructed."

"YOU'VE ALLOWED AN OLD ENEMY TO EMERGE FROM DEATH!"

"An old enemy?"

"YOUR CHILDHOOD FRIEND SEEKS TO DESTROY OUR PLANS, EVEN AS WE SPEAK!"

John thought for a moment. "Arlo? Is it Arlo?"

Balam was silent.

"But I don't get it. How could Arlo . . . I mean, I killed him!"

"YOU DID NOT!"

John lowered his voice. "Please, Lord Balam. Tell me how to defeat him."

"THE ONE YOU CALL ARLO HAS DISCOVERED A NEW PLANE OF EXISTENCE. HE IS EVEN MORE DANGEROUS IN DEATH THAN HE WAS IN LIFE."

"Is there a way to permanently eliminate him?"

Balam remained silent while John began to panic, fearful that he was about to be tortured.

"Wait! I have his mother! Surely, we can use that to our advantage. He loves her, and there is nothing he wouldn't do to make sure she's safe."

"WE WILL ALTER OUR PLANS. TAKE THE CHILDREN TO THE DEATH VALLEY ENTRANCE OF THE UNDERWORLD. WE WILL ASSIMILATE THEM BEFORE THERE IS FURTHER DAMAGE."

"But Lord, I can do this. Please give me an opportunity to—"

"SILENCE! YOU WILL DO AS INSTRUCTED, OR I WILL PERSONALLY DEVOUR YOUR FLESH!"

John obediently lowered his head. "Yes, my Lord."

There was a thunderous boom, and John was back on the stairs of the hospital, staring up at Asura.

"John? Master, are you okay?" asked Asura, leaning over John as he laid on the ground.

John climbed to his feet and wiped the drool from his mouth. "Prepare the aircraft. We'll be taking the children to Death Valley."

Asura looked puzzled. "I'm sorry, I don't understand."

"It seems my old friend Arlo is causing trouble. Lord Balam wants to transport the children to Hell's Gate as soon as possible."

"Arlo? But he's dead. I saw him."

John chuckled. "Arlo was always more intelligent than most people thought. He even outsmarted me with this move."

John turned to face Asura. "You gather the aircraft and figure out a way for us to airlift them out of here. I need to pay a visit to Arlo's mother."

"Why?"

"We need insurance if Arlo decides he wants to be a hero."

32

Eyes in the Sky

As Forneus flew high above the clouds, he searched for an opening that allowed him to pass close to the hospital without being detected. After circling over the patch of black filth in the sky, he saw his opening and swooped down. He immediately saw activity on the hospital lawn and stopped his descent.

"What is going on here?" he whispered.

The children were all standing in a single-file line stretching from the field into the hospital. Meanwhile, the Huturo formed a line on the hospital's perimeter facing the forest.

"They know about us," he added.

Forneus stretched his enormous wings and flew close to the hospital, hoping to see activity inside. After circling the hospital twice, he spotted a woman being led up a staircase with Asura following close behind. Forneus shot high in the sky and hovered behind some rainy clouds. Finally, he spotted several large aircraft on the rooftop. Sitting beside the airplanes were two large cages—one filled with children, and the other with numerous children filing inside.

"They're leaving!"

Forneus's eyes blazed, and he shot up into the clouds. He didn't realize that someone on the ground had noticed his fiery eyes shining in the darkness. John stepped out from the shadows and watched until Forneus was gone.

"That's right," John whispered. "Bring Arlo to me."

33

The Rush to War

Arlo licked the remaining brain matter from inside the cow's skull and tossed it aside. Just as he reached for the cow heart lying on the floor, he paused; the pile of bones on the other side of the room started glowing. Arlo watched as the bones began moving, snapping together like a giant jigsaw puzzle to form the torso of a skeleton. Once assembled, the torso leaned down, and a colossal skull rolled across the floor and attached itself to the wide neck of bones. Slowly, Forneus stood up, and the worms inside his head began squirming, casting an eerie glow on the pile of dead animals in front of Arlo and Isadora.

"We have a problem," said Forneus as he walked over to the pile of rotting meat in front of the teenagers.

"Tell me about it," replied Arlo. "We're in deep shit."

Isadora finished licking a pig skull and tossed the bone aside.

"The shit we saw out there was scary as hell," she said.

Forneus quickly grabbed a pig carcass, ripped the top of its skull off, scooped out a handful of brains, and shoved them into his mouth. Arlo watched as the worms in Forneus's skull wriggled, and the snakes in his chest started to twist in excitement as they digested the meat.

"What did you see?" asked Forneus.

"We were able to kill one of the Huturo," replied Arlo.

Forneus ripped off one of the pig's legs and shoved it in his mouth.

"And?"

"And they transform into something worse."

"Worse?"

"First, the Huturo's bodies melt into a liquid. After a few minutes, the liquid transforms into a gas. Anyone that smells that gas becomes a hideous vampire creature with mouths all over their body."

"Wicked genius."

"Meanwhile, the gas spreads a few feet from the Huturo's body, transforming plants, trees, and wildlife into these strange plants I've never seen before."

"Of course. The Huturo are here to transform Earth into Hell."

"What do we do?"

"Kill as many as possible."

Isadora stood and walked over to Forneus. "Didn't you hear a word we said? If you kill those things, they come back as something much worse. The one we killed is out there killing people and spreading that virus everywhere, and you want to make more of them?"

Forneus sat silently, chewing on his food. "At this point, we do not have another option. War is upon us, whether we choose to accept it or not. Hell is coming, and the only thing we have to fight them with is bone and decaying flesh."

Arlo stood. "What about the women in the forest? They made the Huturo stronger with their sorcery. Maybe they could create a spell to weaken the new creature."

"It's possible. But doing so would surely get the attention of Hell, and I got the feeling the women in the forest don't want confrontation. Some people prefer living in the shadows."

Arlo shrugged. "Who cares? As you said, war is here. Hell is coming to their doorstep, whether they like it or not."

Forneus tossed the empty bone into the pile of carcasses. "There's something else you need to know. John is leaving."

"Leaving?"

"A mass exodus has begun. John is taking the children away."

"To where?"

"My guess? Hell."

"But why?"

"I think they know we're plotting against them. I saw them moving your mother."

Arlo flashed a worried look. "They're taking her to Hell?"

"They're using her as bait to draw you out."

Arlo began trembling and pacing the room. "Well . . . that's my mother. I can't just sit here," he finally replied.

"What do you recommend, Forneus?" asked Isadora.

"We don't have a choice. We must attack now. It's the best opportunity for Arlo to free his mother, and the best opportunity I have to save as many souls as possible. If we allow John to reach Hell with the payload of children, they'll be gone forever, and we'll all be guilty of not trying to free them. Trust me. Heaven will punish us all when it comes to children's souls."

Forneus rose from the ground, grabbed a huge handful of bloody animal entrails, and shoved them into his mouth.

"Take your final bite of food. We leave in two minutes."

34

Twisted Reality

Claire's wet hair stuck to her face like plastic. As the stinging cold rain drenched her body, she stared at the line of emotionless children filing into the cages, and her heart sank. Arlo was somewhere out in the storm, motherless and lost. She tried finding solace in the possibility that her husband, Jamie, was out searching for their son, but she had no way of knowing; Jamie mysteriously disappeared when Manuel and the old woman appeared at their house.

"Manuel," Claire whispered under the howling wind. "Now he's calling himself John."

The thought of such a ridiculous notion both mystified and terrified Claire. What teenage boy would walk around changing their identity? And who was this elderly woman who suddenly appeared at their doorstep in the night? In all the years Claire knew Manuel and his family, she'd never seen this woman. The boy who spent numerous nights playing video games with Arlo was now a frightening enigma, filled with a new maturity she'd never seen, and a coldness in the center of his being that told Claire he was a murderer. She didn't know how to reconcile those facts with what she knew of the boy, but the sinister side of her son's best friend was apparent; Manuel killed people and would kill her if he had to.

Suddenly doubt overcame Claire, and she reached down with her shackled hands and pinched her thigh. Maybe she was imagining all of this and had been in an accident. After all, she was in a hospital. Perhaps she had hit her head and was in an operating room, unconscious and receiving treatment. It could've all started back at the house when she'd seen Arlo as a hideous version of himself.

"Yeah, that's it," Claire whispered before pinching herself again.

Between Arlo's zombie-like appearance and her missing husband, everything made sense now. How else could she explain all this madness? The people out on the lawn with the big eyes and monstrous faces, the headless corpses lying on the hospital floor, the intestines hanging from the ceiling. Claire *had* to be injured. It was either that or lying on the floor, drugged in some mental facility, depressed by her son's disappearance.

Suddenly the hospital door opened, and John walked out with Asura following closely behind. They walked past the deformed child standing guard at the entrance and over to Claire where she stood shackled, leaning against the wall.

"Mrs. Ortega, I hope you can forgive me for keeping you here. Don't worry. We're just waiting for a few more people to be loaded, and then we'll be on our way," said John.

Claire looked at John briefly, then lowered her head.

"Don't you want to know why you're here?" asked John.

"No, Manuel. I don't want to know," she replied.

Asura stepped from behind John. "She misses her son," mumbled Asura.

Claire glanced at the old woman and returned to staring at the puddles on the ground.

John smiled. "Don't worry, Mrs. Ortega. Arlo's going to be—"

Suddenly there was an explosion that shook the whole hospital.

John turned to Asura. "He's here! Are you ready?"

"Yes, John. Everything's in place."

John and Asura ran back into the building, and Claire quickly headed to the rooftop's edge to look below. Thousands of zombies were pouring out of the forests onto the lawn. Claire stumbled back, shaking her head in disbelief.

"What's happening to me?" Claire asked.

The two monsters guarding the exit looked at Claire briefly and turned to one another, speaking in a strange language. Claire started pinching her thigh continuously and shaking her head, refusing to believe what she saw. Suddenly, growling filled the night air, and Claire heard awful screams from the field below. She wanted to run, but there was nowhere to go. Claire's mind began to overload, and she stumbled back to the wall as the whole building shuddered beneath her feet. Claire shot a worried look at the kids piling into the cages; several of them cast a lazy glance toward the rooftop's edge, but none ventured to take a look or even acknowledge Claire.

Slowly, she sank to the ground. Covering her head and sobbing uncontrollably, she blacked out.

35

Attack of the Zombies

Arlo gave the command inside his mind, and the hoard of zombies started pouring onto the field in a mindless rage. There were thousands of them. Some were missing pieces of their faces and body parts, while others were massive hulks of muscle, all running through the toxic rain with their decaying wrinkled flesh shimmering, filled with the desire to eat their enemies' brains.

Meanwhile, Arlo and Isadora waited silently in the shadows, watching. They knew not to run onto the field until there was no other choice; they could feel John in the hospital, looking out of one of the windows, searching for an opportunity to make permanent the death that Arlo had somehow evaded.

As the battle raged, Arlo observed something peculiar; the numerous Huturo posted on the hospital's perimeter seemed confused. Instead of childlike laughter, the monsters seemed startled, racked with uncertainty. They searched for answers amongst each other's faces, seemingly unsure how to respond to the army of zombies sprinting toward them.

The first zombie to reach one of the Huturo was a muscular man with a gaping wound in his torso. The zombie punched the Huturo and used his other hand to dig into one of its eyes. As the Huturo stumbled back with blood and red scorpions covering its face, it became furious, turning to the other creatures and releasing a terrifying growl.

As if they all suddenly understood, the Huturo became raging storms of fury. They jumped on the muscular zombie, tearing and slicing at his torso until his guts fell out of his stomach onto the wet grass. With black fluid leaking from his mouth, the zombie screamed and bit into the head of the closest Huturo. Another Huturo grabbed the man and pulled his head and spine out of his body. With the head still thrashing, attempting to bite the monster, the Huturo heaved the zombie skull into the forest before turning back to confront another creature.

After seeing several of their counterparts ripping the heads off the zombies, the other Huturo began using the same tactic, snatching off zombies' skulls and ripping out their spinal cords. But Arlo noticed the Huturo didn't take the heads and spines into their bodies as they'd done with the humans. Instead, they discarded their handiwork by dropping them where they decapitated their victims, leaving the ground littered with heads. Arlo saw an opportunity. Instead of moving the group away from danger, he implemented a new strategy. For the Huturo closest to the forest, he sent out a message:

"Don't fight," Arlo said in his mind.

He wanted the Huturo to take as many victims as possible. Gradually, the heads and spines began piling up beneath the Huturo.

Arlo flashed a wicked grin at Isadora and kissed her decaying lips. *"Look! Do you see what's happening?"* he asked, pointing to the edge of the battle.

"Yeah! They're fucked!" whispered Isadora.

The heads of the zombies weren't just skulls piling up beneath the feet of the Huturo. They were living, breathing, and biting *weapons.* Arlo understood that the Huturo knew nothing of zombie life and didn't understand that zombies only died from the Sun Oil; all other mortal attacks could only result in injuries. No matter how many zombies the Huturo ripped apart, the undead were still the undead. The never-ending hunger for brains and flesh would continue until they got what they wanted.

The skulls began chewing on the legs of the Huturo, spilling their blood all over the field. And although the scorpions in the Huturo's blood snapped and ripped the skin off the zombies' skulls, the undead continued biting hungrily, chewing, bringing the Huturo to their knees in agony before biting into their torsos.

Still, Arlo continued pushing the zombies to attack. He concentrated his mental energy on directing the murderous mob toward the hospital entrance. With wild eyes, Arlo watched rotting flesh and scorpion-filled blood coat the grass. The horrific screaming and gruesome ripping of organs from the bodies became comforting, music that reminded him they were making progress. With every dead Huturo, Arlo knew he was getting closer to his mom.

"Die," Arlo thought over and over. *"Just die."*

Isadora stared at Arlo, but she knew not to say anything. They only had one chance to reach his mother, and Arlo took the lead.

The zombies tore into the red flesh of the Huturo like jackals on a carcass. With thick goo oozing from their mouths, they bit the skulls of the monsters, attempting to eat their brains. Some were successful and latched onto the Huturo's large heads, sucking until they penetrated, and the beast sank into the mud. Others needed help bringing down the four-armed creatures and waited until other zombies were close enough to initiate a group attack.

Arlo tried guiding the zombies as best he could. When a zombie was struggling, he quickly sent reinforcements to assist. Sometimes he was successful in extracting the danger, but mostly he wasn't. The Huturo were too powerful and promptly ripped off heads like pulling weeds from the ground.

Isadora saw one of the Huturo stiffen and fall to the ground. Seconds later, a glowing purple cloud rose, and the wind blew it toward the hospital.

"Oh, no," said Isadora. *"The kids!"*

Arlo saw the mist and grabbed Isadora's hand. *"Come on! We've got to get to the hospital before that cloud does!"*

Arlo and Isadora sprinted out of the forest and onto the field. As soon as they did, the Huturo were on them; one grabbed Arlo by his head, but Isadora grabbed the creature around its waist and tossed it into a group of zombies.

"This way!" she yelled.

Arlo followed Isadora as she moved through the field, tossing monster after monster, breaking arms with superhuman strength, and punching Huturo like a woman possessed. Arlo kept his eye on the purple cloud while pushing through the attacking monsters. The stormy wind wasn't dissipating the cloud. Instead, the wind seemed to move the blob of poison toward the hospital on an intentional path, growing larger as more Huturo collapsed and died.

"This isn't right. The cloud looks like someone's controlling it," Arlo yelled.

Isadora punched a monster in the mouth. *"Shut up and fight!"* she barked, delivering a vicious kick to the midsection of one of the Huturo.

Arlo grabbed one of the monsters by its head and dug his thumbs into its eyeballs. As soon as he did it, he instantly regretted it; tiny scorpions rushed out of the monster's head and crawled over Arlo's arms.

"Oh, shit!" he yelled, trying to shake them off.

Isadora kicked another one of the Huturo in the face and turned to grab Arlo by his shoulders. She quickly ran her fingers down his arms, removing all the tiny red creatures.

"Come on, Arlo. Stop being fucking stupid. Punch! Hit! But don't draw blood, got it?"

Arlo smiled and hit two approaching monsters in the stomach.

"Damn, Isadora! How'd you get so strong?" he asked.

Isadora didn't respond. Instead, she slid between the legs of one of the Huturo and punched it in the groin. She was unsure if she hurt the creature but was happy when it fell to the ground clutching its privates.

"I guess they do have balls," she said, and laughed.

Finally, the two stood in the middle of the field.

"Do you see that?" asked Arlo, pointing toward the stairs.

Standing in front of the entrance were Asura and John.

"Arlo!" yelled John across the yard. "Is that you?"

Arlo became infuriated. He kicked two Huturo in their teeth and pushed forward through the crowd of monsters. He tried cursing at his friend, but all that came out was a moan—he'd forgotten the difficulties of being a zombie.

"Uhhhhhh," moaned Arlo.

John laughed. "Ahhh, so you do remember me. Good! Don't worry, bro. I *think* I understand what you're trying to say."

Asura quietly moved closer to John and whispered something in his ear. He listened for a moment and then kneeled to touch the ground.

"I'm sorry to do this, dude, but you're not supposed to be here," yelled John.

John grabbed a handful of mud from the ground and shoved it into his mouth. After chewing, he swallowed the muck, and his whole body burst into flame.

Suddenly the ground exploded beneath Arlo's and Isadora's feet and sent them flying through the air.

"Arlo!" cried Isadora as she flew over a group of Huturo.

But Arlo didn't respond. He sailed past a few Huturo and landed facedown in the mud. Arlo immediately rolled over on his back and kicked two approaching Huturo in the face.

Isadora landed on her back and slid into a pile of scorpions—the arachnids came from the blood of one of the injured Huturo lying nearby on the ground. The scorpions jumped on Isadora and began snapping their claws, trying to tear her face apart. But Isadora remained calm, and she quickly brushed the scorpions away. After hitting the injured Huturo again, she sloshed through the mud toward Arlo.

Arlo saw Isadora approaching and rose to his feet. Just as he did, three Huturo came running across the field.

"Isadora! Look out!" screamed Arlo.

Without looking in the Huturo's direction, Isadora ducked and easily avoided the blow from the first creature. Although each Huturo had four arms, Isadora saw this as a weakness. She moved close enough to one of the Huturo's rib cage without letting the monster's arms touch her. When the other Huturo tried to grab her, Isadora ducked behind the first Huturo's torso, causing their arms to become entangled. She jumped in the air and delivered perfectly timed punches to all three of the creature's faces, sending them tumbling to the ground like a house of cards.

"I have someone I want you to meet!" yelled John, his body covered in flame.

Suddenly the mud beneath Arlo's and Isadora's feet began bubbling.

"What the hell is this?" asked Isadora.

Arlo felt something moving the mud. He quickly brushed aside a patch of soil and saw a red thumbnail.

He turned to Isadora. *"Run!"*

The two teenagers took one step, but a shudder beneath the field shook everything, and they both fell to the ground.

"Arlo!" yelled Isadora.

Suddenly the ground exploded, drenching both teens in filth and leaving an enormous hole in the center of the lawn. Arlo inched close to the edge of the pit and looked inside. The black smoke was thick inside the hole, but Arlo saw something deep inside—two enormous glowing red eyes staring back at him. He was about to run when he spotted another pair of eyes watching him. Then suddenly, as if Arlo awakened what was inside, hundreds of eyes opened and rushed toward him. Arlo turned to run, but a shiny black hand filled with dozens of rocklike fingers reached out and grabbed his ankle.

"AHHHHHH!" Arlo screamed.

The gigantic hand was like acid; it melted Arlo's pants and stripped the skin from his leg. Arlo kicked himself free of the creature's grasp, melting his shoe. The monster reached up again but grabbed the edges of the pit this time. Isadora ran to Arlo's side and watched as multiple shiny black human arms appeared on the pit's edge. Finally, after six different hands grabbed the edge of the hole, a rush of air came out of the pit, and the creature shot out of the hole. It landed on the ground in front of the teenagers.

"No!" whispered Arlo.

Standing in front of Arlo was a half-human, half-spider. In the center of the creature on a human torso was a shiny black demonic, charred face with horns. Piled behind it were dozens of corpses, all humans, with glowing red eyes. They all were alive, moving independently behind the main Demon, mimicking his angry expressions, growling, biting, and snapping their mouths at everything around them. All the bodies sat atop the shiny black body of a spider with dozens of legs made of lava moving beneath it.

The main Demon looked at the ground and saw the skin from Arlo's leg in the mud. With one of its arms, it grabbed the sheath of skin, tossed it in the air, and shredded it. With its arms, the monster snatched the pieces of skin from the air. It shoved the skin into the mouths of the various corpses and closed its eyes, waiting for each monster to consume Arlo's flesh. Finally, it flashed a sinister smile.

"You will be an excellent fit for us," all the human heads said in unison.

Isadora looked toward the stairs and saw John and Asura disappearing inside. She quickly looked up and saw the cloud of poison approaching the entrance.

"Arlo! They're getting away! We're almost out of time!"

The Spider Demon frowned at Isadora and crawled across the grass toward her.

"Isadora!" Arlo yelled.

Isadora saw the spider approaching from the corner of her eye. She ran to the nearest Huturo, grabbed one of its legs, and hurled it toward the Spider Demon. The Demon avoided the Huturo and opened its mouth, shooting webbing made of fire at Isadora. The teenager avoided the web of fire, and it landed on a group of Huturo, killing them and releasing the violet fog from their burning corpses. The Spider Demon leaped into the air and was about to pounce on Isadora when it froze mid-air. The creature started trembling, and the Spider Demon's bodies began shrieking.

"Free us!"

"We are not your enemies!"

"He made us do it!"

"Hell is a devil!"

Soon a pink bubble enveloped the Spider Demon, and it began moving back toward the hole. Arlo looked around, startled. Finally, his eyes fell on the source of their good luck—Penny, one of the three sorceresses. A long chain of pink energy stretched from her fingertips to the Spider Demon, dragging it back to the hole.

Arlo flashed a smile at the girl.

"Forneus told us you needed help, so I'm here. My sisters didn't want to get involved, but I couldn't resist the opportunity to pay back that bitch Asura!" said Penny.

Isadora jumped to her feet and ran past Arlo. "Come on! We don't have much time left!"

Arlo jumped up, too, and ran behind Isadora. Just as they arrived at the stairs, the cloud of poisonous gas reached the entrance, and something sucked it inside.

"No!" screamed Isadora. "We're too late!"

Arlo fell to his knees. "Mooooooom!"

As they stood watching the door, they saw the silhouette of a child in the fog. Slowly, the child emerged from the smoke, and Arlo's heart sank—the child had thousands of mouths all over its bod. It was a vampire.

"Come on, baby," whispered Isadora, pulling Arlo away from the entrance. "Let's get out of here before they all come out of the hospital.

Reluctantly, Arlo turned away from the hospital and back toward the yard of Huturo.

"See you soon, Mom," Arlo whispered.

There was the flapping of wings overhead, and Arlo looked up to see a large bird with blazing eyes. Arlo gave the command inside his mind, and the zombies on the field started stumbling back into the forest.

Arlo grabbed Isadora by her hand. *"Thanks for being here with me,"* he said.

Isadora chuckled. *"I said the same thing to you. Remember?"*

Arlo smiled and wrapped his arm around her waist. Suddenly the colossal bird lifted them in its vast talons and flew toward the forest. As the bird took the two zombies away, Penny threw the angry Spider Demon into its hole and piled dirt on it. After shooting several Huturo with her magic, she sealed the chasm in the field and disappeared.

36

The Getaway

Asura moved quickly through the hospital with John following closely behind. After riding the elevator to the next level, they climbed the rooftop stairs.

"Is the cargo loaded?" John asked.

"Yes, Lord. The mist will transform the remaining stragglers."

"Good. Balam will be pleased."

Asura opened the door to the roof and froze. There were thousands of cherry blossom flowers all over the rooftop. Terrified, Asura looked up and saw cherry blossoms raining from the sky.

"My Lord, we must go!" she said, pulling John back toward the exit.

"What?" asked John. "What are you talking about?"

Trembling uncontrollably, Asura spun around as if she were lost. She looked up at the sky, and her face twisted in agony. The flowers were falling more rapidly now, coating everything on the rooftop. The smell of lilac was heavy in the air, rushing into her nostrils and making her want to vomit. Asura turned to John to speak, and one of the cherry blossoms landed on her tongue.

"Oh!" Asura yelped, wiping her mouth and spitting it on the ground.

John stared in disbelief. He could see that the event bothered Asura —terrified her, even. She was almost beside herself, chanting under her breath and quickly removing any flower that landed in her hair. In all the years Asura had been with John, he had never seen the old woman appear so weak and out of control, trembling like a flower in the rain.

"Asura, what's wrong?" asked John.

But Asura wasn't there. It was as though the person standing before him was a stranger John had never known. Asura was frantic and growing more so by the second. Her smooth brown skin now looked like an old, used, faded towel. When she started wheezing, John grabbed her by the shoulders and slapped her face.

"What is this, Asura? Get a hold of yourself! What the hell is going on?"

Asura looked up into the sky and saw rays of light piercing the dark clouds. She quickly looked around and spotted Claire cowering in the corner.

"Come with me! Now!" Asura yelled at Claire.

Claire looked up at the strange old lady, tears streaming down her face.

"Who are you? Are you a nurse?"

"Get up, you bitch!" snapped Asura, grabbing the distraught woman by her hair.

"Ow! Let go of me!" screamed Claire.

Asura dragged the prisoner across the roof to her master. "Lord, we must go! They're coming!"

Suddenly a deep thunder rumbled in the clouds. The sound startled John, and he looked up at the sky, confused.

"What are all these flowers? Who's coming?"

"Can't you see? The Angels! They're here!"

Suddenly the clouds exploded in a brilliance that lit up the rooftop. Asura grabbed John's arm, kicked open the door, and pushed him inside. Just as she dragged Claire into the building by her hair, the clouds exploded, and three winged, faceless figures appeared.

Asura quickly searched the rooftop until she spotted the two deformed creatures standing guard over the children.

"Ton-kabin-eashi!" she yelled to the monsters before entering the building and slamming the door.

The words ignited a reaction inside the monsters, and they turned to roar at the approaching figures covered in light. The children in the cages screamed as the creatures began changing; unsightly bumps suddenly appeared all over their bodies, and the faces that hung down began moving like something inside was trying to get out.

As the Angels drifted down, one of them extended a palm, and a burst of snow blanketed the children on the rooftop, freezing them like statues.

The two monsters rushed forward, and their disfigured faces split, revealing one giant red eye inside their bodies. Continuous bursts of flame shot from their eyes at the descending Angels, but the fire passed through the heavenly creatures without touching them. The Angels pointed at the monsters with their index fingers, and a blue laser hit the two monsters in their foreheads. The light lifted the monsters off the ground and made them convulse, screaming as the blue light lit up their bodies. Suddenly two glass figures shaped like children emerged from the twisted flesh, floated across the roof, and landed beside the others.

The remaining flesh was evil, still living, twisting itself into various shapes, unable to take solid form. The monstrous blobs growled at the Angels like angry dogs, furious at being deprived of their hosts. One of the Angels calmly flew closer to the monsters. Wings flapping, the Angel held up its hand, and suddenly two enormous thunderbolts shot out of its palm. The thunderbolts didn't make a sound as they flew to the chest of their targets, but when they hit, a tremendous thunder rumbled in the sky, causing the building to shake. Both creatures turned to dust and blew away in the breeze.

The Angels landed on the rooftop and ran to the edge of the building to look down. Surveying the area, the Angels waved their hands and suddenly their faces appered.

"All clear," said Malaika. "It looks like there are a couple of hundred of the Huturo on the ground.

Jamison walked to the frozen children, and his eyes began glowing; suddenly the snow melted away, and the children started moving again. Jamison walked to a little girl and ran his palm along the top of her head, pushing away chunks of ice. The little girl looked up at him slowly and smiled.

"I'll take care of the baby souls," he said. "You two go down and banish the Huturo."

"What about John?" asked Haleena.

"They won't get far," replied Jamison.

"And Arlo?" asked Malaika.

Jamison flapped his wings and whipped up the cherry blossom petals lying on the roof.

"He's the biggest priority. We have to find him first."

Malaika and Haleena ran to the edge of the building and jumped over. There was a whooshing sound, and the two Angels were soaring in the air with multicolored wings. They each passed their hands in front of their faces and their features melted away, replaced by a plain white veil of light. The Huturo on the ground beneath them looked up at the Angels in the sky and screamed. Some ran into the forest while others stood frozen in fear; some let their arms drop and transform into monstrous scorpions. But all reactions were futile. Malaika and Haleena were too powerful—they rained down silent thunderbolts on the monsters with such accuracy, none could escape. As soon as the electricity hit the creatures, they vaporized, leaving nothing but cherry blossom petals where they'd once stood. The Angel's arms hurled so many thunderbolts at the monsters that their arms blurred. There was no sound as the lightning struck the beasts, but the sky above them crackled and rumbled like it was falling.

Meanwhile, Jamison stood on the rooftop attending to the children. The rumbling of the sky frightened them, and they were out of their minds with fear.

"Shhhhh," Jamison said. He used his powers to drown out the thunder by flapping his wings fast. Soon his wings were moving so fast, they appeared stationary, and an invisible bubble formed over the rooftop, blocking all sound. Soon the kids were smiling at the Angel with purple eyes and a radiant smile.

"Mommy? Where's my mommy?" asked a little girl.

"Where's my dad?" asked a boy.

"I want to go home," cried another boy.

The Angel walked toward the terrified children.

"Come with me, babies," his soft voice said. "I'll take you home."

Jamison turned away from the children, looked up into the dark sky, and opened his arms. In an instant, the gray clouds began rumbling and changing shapes. Sparks of lightning shot across the sky until, finally, the poisonous clouds disappeared, melting away like a giant hand wiping away filth from a smog-stained window. In their place appeared white and blue nebulas filled with water.

Soon a cool mist started falling from the sky, and all the children held up their hands to catch the sweet liquid. Several children opened their mouths and let the rain land on their tongues. The children's bond with nature made the Angel happy, and he smiled at the sight of the act. He knew the hardship the children had experienced, and he understood the joy in their hearts, the feeling of happiness at triumphing over despair, to know that the sun existed and that everything was going to be alright. It was a connection that God put in all living things, and it was nice to see the bond still strong after evil attempted to unravel it.

A tiny girl began to hum a song and, like magic, a rainbow stretched across the sky. The children smiled as they looked from the face of the kind man to the beautiful colors painted on the canvas above them. The dreariness was gone. The cold, empty feeling inside htheir souls that made them weary became a distant memory. Now all they saw was the sun, the rainbow, and the billowy clouds that danced between them—the brilliant ball of happiness shining on faces.

Suddenly Jamison's body began to glow as he stood in front of the children. But the kids didn't turn away. Instead, they moved closer to him. Soon the brilliance surrounding Jamison's body made it impossible for the children to see him. Still, they held out their tiny arms, trying to touch him. One by one, they walked into his body, smiling and filled with laughter.

"Home," Jamison whispered.

He located the family members of each child and sent them there. The Huturo had extinguished the light of so many of their parents that there was no other choice. The mothers and fathers were gone.

Jamison walked to the roof's edge when the last child was gone and looked at the field. The other Angels were battling the Huturo and winning.

"So much anger and evil," he whispered.

Jamison flapped his enormous wings and shot into the sky. He hovered over the field, watching quietly as the Angels shot thunderbolts into the fleeing monsters. When the Angels killed the last Huturo, Jamison landed on the field and walked to the forest's edge.

"Is he in there?" asked Haleena.

"Yes," replied Jamison. "But I feel something more sinister inside."

"Forneus, maybe?" said Malaika.

Jamison moved closer to the darkness, and a gust of cold wind blew out of the forest, making his wings shiver.

"No. This evil is something different."

"Should we seek guidance from the Halls before entering?"

"There isn't enough time. We must convince Arlo to turn away from his sinful existence in the undead realm before it's too late. Our presence here has alerted Hell of his importance, and they, too, will send their soldiers to convince him to give his soul to their cause."

Malaika flapped her wings and walked into the forest. "Let's get him," she said as she disappeared into the darkness.

Jamison and Haleena cast worried looks at one another before following Malaika into the dark forest.

Milton Keynes UK
Ingram Content Group UK Ltd.
UKHW021928261023
431418UK00005B/55